FLIRTING WITH DISASTER

A Noble Pass Affaire Novella

A Noble Pass Affaire Novella Series

Flirting with Fire by Misty Dietz

Flirting with Disaster by Josie Matthews

Flirting with Sin by Naima Simone

Flirting with Fate by Jerrie Alexander

Flirting with the Devil by Kym Roberts

Coming Soon from Josie Matthews

Crazy For Loving You

A Noble Pass Affaire Novella

FLIRTING with Disaster

JOSIE MATTHEWS

A Josie Matthews Publication

FLIRTING WITH DISASTER

Josie Matthews Publishing
September 2015
Print ISBN: 978-0-9965550-0-5
Electronic ISBN: 978-0-9965550-1-2

Cover Illustrator: Misty Dietz,
   www.MistyDietz.com
Edited by: A.J. Nuest,
   www.AJNuest.com
Interior Design by: Top-ePublishing Services,
   www.Top-ePublishingServices.com

Acknowledgements

So many people to acknowledge and thank for their support, guidance and encouragement. It takes a diehard team to create a few moments of feel-good fantasy for my readers.

To my family: Thanks for staring at the back of my head and realizing I didn't hear a word you said while I was writing.

To Mom and Dad: For your belief and support over the years.

To my most awesome editor, A.J. Nuest: You have the patience of all the saints combined, and a kick-ass sense of exactly what I need.

To my Chick Swagger sisters, Misty, Kym, Jerrie, A.J., and Naima: Thanks for your unending patience, support, and guidance through this process.

Thanks to my critique partners, Misty, Jo, and Rachel who always steer me in the right direction when I get antsy!

A big hug to my Chick Swagger Sirens Street Team for their awesome support!

To Char and Shelly: Thanks for your humor, support and invaluable input through my imaginings.

For Michael, since he wouldn't read it until he could buy it.

One

*"Anyone who has never made a mistake
has never tried anything new."
Albert Einstein*

"How many calories are in a…Screaming Orgasm?" Jude Duffy glanced at the young man behind the bar in hopes of some guidance. "No, wait…what about the Bend Over Shirley? Could I have that with seltzer instead of Sprite? Or the Mickey Slim, maybe?"

She returned the drink list to the bar. "I knew a man named Mickey once. He attended one of my studies regarding the hormonal imbalances of mono-zygotic twins in relationship to the concordance for homosexuality."

Alas, Jude wouldn't likely experience the

sterile safety of her precious lab ever again.

She sighed and slid the resort brochure from her purse. Castle Alainn in October, A Mystical Adventure. Jude snorted. This whole vacation/contest win, organized by her dear Aunt Agnes before her death a month ago, was nothing but a frivolous excursion to help Jude forget the most humiliating moment of her life. And she hated frivolity. It was a threat to her safety and the safety of those around her. She was not a frivolous type of being if one considered her PhD, her Chevy Spark Hatchback, and the 401K she'd invested in since she was sixteen.

The bartender's brows lifted. "Honey, how about we start with a nice Long Island Iced Tea?" The room echoed with the delight of other patrons, muffling the bartender's comments. "You look a little…uptight."

Jude relaxed a bit on the bar stool. "Yes, an iced tea would be lovely." A simple iced tea for an unfamiliar experience. Perfect. "Is your water filtered? I'd prefer spring water, if that's okay?" He smiled and turned away. She reached into her purse for an antibacterial wipe, cleansed her hands and the bar surface before tucking the wipe safely into the sleeve of her cardigan.

The place *was* beautiful. Exposed beams, luxurious couches, and ornate chandeliers. This castle resort in Noble Pass, Colorado was known for its reclusive opulence—owned by an eclectic Irish couple who organized a ridiculous "Noble Pass Affaire" contest each month. And the prize? A week's stay to give a failure like her a break from her unpalatable state of affairs.

Too bad October's win had been wasted on a thirty-eight-year-old, misanthropic virgin like her.

"Here you go, Sweetie."

Jude glanced at the bartender's name tag. "Thank you, Steven."

He nodded then winked and walked away. She sipped from the tall crystal glass, the sweet, pungent flavor tweaking her taste buds while she admired the rustic architecture of the room.

That horrid *Harry Strubel Show* would air across the country tonight. When Evan, her ex-fiancé, had introduced her to the producers of the famous talk show three months ago, she'd been under the impression she was to appear to discuss her anthropological studies. The ones she'd been conducting with her research team to debunk the antagonistic myths for the causes of homosexuality.

Instead, she'd been used as nothing but a prop for a comedic debacle involving her fiancé...*and* his newly acquired Latin lover.

She'd been so imbecilic. Evan had been perfect during their three year engagement, but Jude should've listened when her lab partner had voiced her concerns over Evan's uncanny ability to yard sale for hours on end, and the fact he wore eyeliner...sometimes.

Jude had just figured he was inextricably in touch with his feminine side, a metro sexual. But her foresight and intelligence had been sabotaged by her innate yearning to be a mother, have a family.

Harry Strubel had to point out her pedantic impotence, her complete deficiency in the face of her fellow anthropologists—on national television—by having Evan announce he was leaving her for the effeminate Timothy Cammarerra, her wedding planner. She sincerely hoped Timothy dumped Evan one day for an androgynous hooker from Henry Street. After tonight's airing, she'd forever be known as the "Honey, you're nice, but I like his package better than yours" girl.

God, the humiliation.

She sipped from her second iced tea—

Steven was so obliging and prompt with his refills—and glanced toward the couple two stools down. The male was going to leave his partner. The body language, the incongruity of their appearances, the apathetic physiognomy...love was a game for fools.

Jude had been more in love with the idea of being married so she could start a family—something she'd never had—than she'd ever been in love with Evan.

It was tough to love a man who had better eyebrows than her.

She cringed and stirred her iced tea. Maybe she should've gone with the Rocky Mountain Bear Fucker. She needed something strong and alcoholic to numb the shame. Plain old iced tea just wasn't cutting it.

Nine-fifty. Ten minutes until her national humiliation, the end of her career, the end of any credibility she'd ever had in the world of science. How had she not known? Had she been so out of touch with her own life, she'd not even noticed the signs?

She snorted. More likely, she'd just chose to ignore them in the arbitrary pursuit of some diaphanous dream of love, family...belonging. Maybe she needed a change in her life.

5

Jude scanned the bar. No televisions, thank goodness. No one here would recognize her. Except maybe that dark, mysterious creature skulking in the corner like he was one of the damned.

She sipped her drink and squinted. He looked dangerous. Maybe he was a plant by the castle owners. A brooding, enigmatic monster to add some whimsy to the Halloween season.

She glanced back at the flyer on the bar. *Mystical Adventure.*

From the looks of it, Mr. Mystical, Dark, and Handsome was contemplating murder over a scotch. He wore all black with a messy length of hair accented by a widow's peak.

Dracula, yes. He would be Dracula tonight.

He turned and glowered in her direction, and her gaze drifted to the long, ragged scar down his left cheek. He didn't look amicable. More spine-chilling in an I-want-to-eat-you kind of way.

Typical, provocative specter material.

She shivered. Definitely *The Beast* of Castle Alainn.

"Steven, I'll have another, please. These are quite refreshing. Do you use an herbal tea?" The words had some trouble exiting her tongue. Steven just smiled and left to fill her order.

Nine-fifty-nine. Maybe Evan would stab himself in the privates with one of his knitting needles. She snorted and iced tea shot from her nose. She grabbed a napkin and held it to her face, torn between laughing and crying.

He'd used her. Used her on national television to catapult his nonexistent acting career. He'd be famous after this. And she'd be ruined.

She glanced at the grand clock behind the bar. Her heart raced and her breathing became labored. Tears swelled in her eyes.

"You need help, miss?"

Jude stiffened. That deep rasp sent chills down her body like a good head massage at the hairdressers. She wiped at her tears with the sleeve of her cardigan. "Only if you happen to have a shotgun with a real strong scope."

"I left it in my pickup with some roadkill I picked up for dinner and a carton of unfiltered Camels."

She turned and encountered…*The Scarred Beast.* Her breath caught at his sheer masculine beauty, despite the jagged scar running from his temple to his chin and marring his high cheekbone. His eyes were the color of rich whiskey, reflecting the candlelight in the room. And his hair… A decadent, wavy brown that beckoned her fingers.

His angled brows lowered over those ethereal, piercing eyes. "What's his name?"

Jude gaped, transfixed. He was doing that mind trick thing vampires did. She was sure of it. "I call him Asshole," she muttered.

The Beast smirked. Not an amiable smirk, by any means, the left side of his mouth slightly crooked from the scar. "I'm sure."

"Here's your drink, miss," Steven interrupted.

Beast continued to stare into her eyes, doing his mind trick thing, keeping her captivated with his savage beauty. "That will be enough, Steven. Ms.…?"

"D…Darling…" She couldn't dare tell anyone her real name for fear of connecting her with *The Harry Strubel Show*.

"Ms. *Darling* has had more than enough." Her false name poured from his beautiful lips like smooth, heated rum…with a twist of suspicious intuition.

Something in the back of her muddled mind protested. "On the contrary, Steven. Thank you very much." She grabbed the glass while glaring into those vampire eyes, wiped blindly at the rim with her napkin to be sure it was relatively clean, and chugged.

She slammed the glass down on the bar and folded her hands in her lap. Hopefully, she hadn't dripped any on her Brunello Cucinelli, organza, waterfall maxi.

"I hope you enjoyed that. Those drinks contain about five shots of liquor."

"Nonsenssse." She flicked her wrist at the young bartender. "Steven has made me a special iced tea, knowing I'm from New York. Are the tea leaves grown on Long Island?"

Steven smiled as he washed a glass. "No, but the alcohol may have been distilled there."

Her mouth dropped as The Beast's smirk widened into a full-out, condescending grin. His teeth were remarkably white—Hollywood, toothpaste-ad, white. She squinted and looked a little closer at his canines for extrusive points. "Are you a…vampire?" she slurred.

Jude Duffy never slurred her words. She hiccupped, and quickly covered her mouth.

Maybe The Beast/Count could use those beautiful, sharp, white teeth on Evan's cheating penis.

She laughed into her hand. Needing a respite, she stood to leave, but her foot tangled with the leg of the stool. Her body tilted, the floor approached...

A muscular arm wrapped around her waist and righted her descent.

Nailed it.

His alluring scent wrapped her in a cocoon of seduction that was completely unfamiliar. "Maybe I should escort you."

Escort. Is that what Count Vampire was? A male escort supplied by the Castle to entertain plain, boring spinsters like her? "Is that your game, sir? Are you planning on taking advantage of me, by ravishing me to satisfy your primal urges for sexual satiation?"

His grin mocked her. Her hand rose to touch the offensive brute's bladed, scarred cheekbone, an insatiable need to assess the contradiction of perfection and destruction. His features froze, a portrait of impassioned torment. She quickly recovered and clenched her fingers.

He stepped back, the movement so fluid she

was momentarily drawn toward him. "No ravishing tonight, Ms. Darling," he stated blandly. "Consider me only your polite escort. Management rules."

Jude tried to organize his words in her foggy brain, but she kept getting mired in his thick, masculine purr. "So, you're an escort? A male escort? And you are rejecting me based on management rules?"

Her virgin-self, damned the management. So unlike her. Dr. Jude Duffy was polite, polished, and poised. She tucked a fallen lock of hair back into her tight bun. Her life was perfectly ordered. It was safest that way.

"It's for the best." His features gave nothing of his thoughts away. "Trust me."

"Fine." Insulted, she slung her Nina Ricci bucket bag over her shoulder. She took one step and found the floor wasn't as level as she'd expected. It *was* an old castle.

Count Beast steadied her again with the agility of an athlete. His touch electrified her. The tingling vectors shot through her body like a lightning storm. It was…mystifying. Familiar in a way no stranger's touch should be, yet utterly compelling. She melted into his arms, wanting to stay there forever, his spicy scent enveloping her in a fog of comfort, need, and...*lust*.

Just how un-orderly *could* the resident gigolo, Beast-Count make her life? Because, incontestably, order and management hadn't done *shit* for her up to this point.

She righted herself and teetered toward the exit before any other frivolous, foreign feelings invaded.

A burst of laughter shot from a group of three couples, sitting abreast the huge stone fireplace, surveying a cell phone in harmony. "How the hell did she not know? Just look at him. He's wearing blush and he's prettier than my first wife!"

She stopped in her tracks and her ass landed on the nearest barstool. "Steven! Another iced tea, please. No, scratch that. I need something stronger. Give me that Screaming Orgasm from a Fucking Rock Bear!"

And Jude Duffy never cursed.

Two

"Everything that can be counted does not necessarily count; everything that counts cannot necessarily be counted."
Albert Einstein

Wh	at the hell was *she* doing here?

Fate was a villainous bitch.

Beckette Slader let the cold water cascade over his body, hoping it would calm the massive erection he'd acquired ever since meeting prim, proper, Jude Darling Duffy.

He'd recognized her immediately, but he had no business approaching her tonight. No right to infect her life, once again, with the specter of his noxiousness. That was his cross to bear.

He'd ruined her future long ago, unbeknownst to her. He wouldn't do it again.

So why had he approached her? Why was he so drawn to her after only one, short meeting?

He'd never been attracted to gingers. He hadn't been attracted to any woman in forever. That flaming red hair, bolted to her head like a sniper's helmet. How was it she didn't have a massive headache? The pale skin, the freckles— he hated freckles—and those slanty green eyes? She resembled an evil, orange tabby.

What the fuck had he been thinking?

His erection throbbed. He had to stop obsessing over a woman he didn't even know. It was diabolical. He'd been celibate for twelve months—as long as he'd been sober—because sex and alcohol had just gone together for him.

The alcohol had helped him forget his cursed past, and the sex had naturally followed. A "Hail Mary" attempt to feel something— anything—again. Now, tonight, the torrid emotions running through his veins were so foreign and ludicrous, he had to wonder about the stories Alana and Liam had told him about the castle. The secret powers it had to grant the residents' deepest desires. The ghosts.

In this moment, the most urgent desire he had, was to get off.

He grabbed his cock and went at it, thinking about her. That smart mouth, those plump lips wrapped around him, instead of his raspy, callused hand. Those gorgeous eyes staring up at him with trust and love.

He laughed at those two words, then came harder than he had in ages. He couldn't be trusted. He didn't trust himself, not to slide back into the clutches of alcoholism, destroying people's lives again.

Like he'd destroyed Jude's, all those years ago.

And Elizabeth's.

He'd started drinking to fill the gaping wounds of an emotionally abusive father. Sadly, the alcohol bored holes in every part of his life, and had failed to fill his sorrow.

But that was the past. He had to move on and stop blaming Dad for all his shit. He'd finally been given a second chance at rekindling his acting career.

Immersing himself in the numbing hours of pretending to be someone else, would keep him from his demons. This lead in an upcoming motion picture would be his big break, after years of landing weak roles in daytime soaps because of his riotous reputation. The producers of the new vampire-themed movie were willing to give him a chance, but they wanted a respectable professional for the romantic lead.

He'd been nothing but a drunk, violent storm the last six years, ever since Elizabeth had died, and this twelve month hiatus was almost over. Much longer away from the screen and he'd be forgotten by his public, obsolete. He only had so much time to clean up his act.

Getting his career back on track meant he could go back to ignoring the pain. All work and no play, would make Beck a dull boy, but he'd be a sober dull boy. He'd be able to forget who and what he was.

A monster.

That was the sole reason he'd changed his name seventeen years ago. A decision forced by his father, so Beck wouldn't bring any more shame to his family after the accident that ruined Jude Duffy's life, and started his descent toward self-destruction. Fine by him. He didn't want anyone delving into his past. Gabriel Beckette Slauter did not exist anymore. Not to him, and not to his family. Only the phantom, Beckette Slader, remained.

Beck finished his shower and dressed for

bed. He bunked in the lower level since he was only staff. The place suited him—cold, bleak, alone...haunted. His AA sponsor figured doing a little grunge work would help him "find himself." His agent had suggested volunteering for this twelve month, maintenance man stint at Castle Alainn—which supported many non-profit organizations similar to his own, Angel Wings—would help his recovery and endear him to the producers of Dark Hallows.

All the freaking restraint of the past twelve months was probably why he couldn't get Ms. Jude Duffy out of his mind.

He needed to get laid.

He didn't do relationships anymore. He just needed a good fuck. 'Cause there were no such things as fairy-tale spells, and curses that granted secret desires. If there were, he'd have no dark past to keep from her, no daily recovery to saddle her with. And he'd have her here, writhing in his arms, while he fucked her senseless and kept her safe from assholes like himself.

Naive women like Jude Duffy, knew nothing of the games damaged men could play, and they could not be left to their own devices. They needed to be saved, but he'd be damned if he was the one for the job.

He was no savior.

No, quite the opposite.

He was a murderer.

Three

*"Only two things are infinite, the universe
and human stupidity, and I'm not sure
about the former."*
Albert Einstein

Someone had poured a box of stale baking soda in Jude's mouth and her stomach was not happy about it.

She gingerly rolled over to the crackle of crunchy sheets. Everything hurt and, as the room spun, her belly contested. Something poked her back. She reached underneath her and pulled out a wrinkled Almond Joy wrapper.

She loved Almond Joys, but hadn't had one in over a year. Not since her diet...since losing thirty pounds, since becoming the ignoramus anthropologist studying homosexuality, who didn't know her own fiancé was gay.

"You look…nice."

The feminine voice came from the entryway to the beautiful suite she'd been assigned. Jude risked opening one eye and found a tiny, twenty-something girl with black, pixie-ish hair smiling down at her.

"I don't feel nice."

"No, I don't imagine you do. Almond Joys?"

Jude managed to swallow, regardless of the absence of saliva in her mouth. "They're like Mounds, but with little, nutty bundles of happiness stuck inside. I love Almond Joys." She sighed.

"Yes, I can see that." The girl's smile was sheerly radiant. She stuck out her hand. "Nola Stonewater. I'll be your maid and assistant during your stay."

"Jude, Jude Duffy…*previously* known as Dr. Duffy. Why are you in my room, witnessing my unabridged demoralization, instead of outside knocking like a normal maid?"

"You didn't answer my knock, so I assumed you were out."

Jude lifted her head and squinted at the clock, the green blur reminding her of a certain misplaced, angry glare. She frowned, vaguely remembering *The Beast* from last night. Put any man with a morose, chiseled face in a black turtle neck, black pants, and a dark room and he'd look like Dracula. Especially if one had a few too many Long Island Iced Teas. "What time is it?"

"Time for you to get up. You're in the castle of secret desires, you know. You won this contest. It's time you enjoyed it."

Jude pulled the pillow over her head and rolled away from her tormentor. "I don't believe in secrets, or desires, or enjoyment. My life is over."

The bed sank under the weight of Jude's perky maid. Jude didn't like perky. She only liked Almond Joys.

"If it's over, that means you get to start again. Out with the old Ms. Duffy and in with the new."

Jude sat up a little too quickly. Her stomach knotted as bile screamed up the back of her throat. She scrambled out of bed and ran past the fireplace to the large, tiled bathroom. She slammed the door on her self-appointed "Fairy Godmaid", and tried in vain to vomit.

This was why she hated frivolity. It was unsafe and likely to produce vomiting.

She hung over the doubtlessly germ-infested toilet, no sanitizing wipes in sight. Chaos, anarchy, pandemonium…they all brought destruction. And she'd had enough destruction in her life.

What had happened last night? Had she actually hungered to sleep with a total stranger? The thought was preposterous. She sighed and rested her head on her forearm. The thought was…freeing.

"You okay? I could get you a few more Almond Joys, if you'd like." Nola's lilting voice beckoned through the thick mahogany door. Jude sat back on the black and white mosaic tiled floor, and leaned against the wall. Maybe a nice bath in the claw-foot tub would calm her.

She smiled. The thought brought on images of her spinster Aunt Agnes—the woman who'd sent Jude here as her dying wish. The woman who had taken her in when she was seventeen, ever since the day her famous rock and roll parents had died in that horrific plane crash—on their way to another tour, another adrenaline rush, another journey in search of fame and glory.

Away from her.

Fame had taken them from her, month after month. Right up until the day they'd died.

And then there was Evan, leaving her alone, humiliating her for the sake of a boost in his acting career.

She hated fame and all those who heeded the calling. People who needed the attention and adoration of total strangers to feel good about themselves.

"Hey! You coming out, or are you staying in there the whole week?"

Fairy Godmaid. Jude would've loved to stay in the opulent bathroom for the whole week. She could survive here…with enough Almond Joys. But that was cowardly. And Jude Duffy had been cowardly far too long.

She rose off the floor and bent over the sink to wash her face. She dropped her head and drank from the faucet. She'd hit an all-time low.

The door opened behind her.

"I'm almost done," she gurgled. "I'll be right out."

"I hope you're not done, 'cause if you go out looking like that, you'll scare the shit out of the other guests."

Jude jolted, keeping her head in the sink, her lips at the faucet. That was not the melodic voice of her Fairy Godmaid. That was the voice of pure malevolent sin.

The Beast.

"I wanted to check and make sure you were okay this morning."

Jude lifted her head and squinted at his reflection in the mirror. He still looked magnificent. His eyes were brighter than she remembered, a shocking amber-gold framed by chiseled, impassive features.

"Are you one of those natural-type girls who doesn't bathe or shave, thinking you're savin' the environment?"

Her gaze shifted to her own reflection…

"Shit! Get out! Now!" She slammed the door and rested her back against it, risking another glance at her reprehensible appearance. Her normally tamed, mechanically straightened hair was frizzled, tangled, and practically undulating on the right side. The left side was matted flat, an Almond Joy wrapper stuck with a bit of leftover chocolate. Probably the same chocolate that was stuck on her left cheek.

Frivolity sucked.

Nola pushed her way in. "He's gone. You can come out now."

Odd how, in her lowest moment of fragmentation and debasement, a Fairy Godmaid was comforting. Must've been the leftover alcohol numbing her intelligence and pragmatic fortitude.

"It's okay. Cross my heart, it's just you and me. He was just stopping by after he left Miss Carmichael's room this morning."

Jude snorted. *Figures.* Professional, hot, male-escort-vampire had turned down frumpy her last night for… "Ms. Carmichael." She sneered. They'd probably done all sorts of nasty, sexual, *beastly* things. Things she knew nothing about.

She'd done what? Saved her virginity for the man she was going to marry? A gay man?

Jude shook her head and sidestepped her way past Nola to the closet. She flung hangers side to side, looking for something to wear for lunch.

Nola pulled the Almond Joy wrapper from Jude's hair. "The castle is rumored to be haunted in October, you know."

The tilted grin and raised brows on her

maid's face made Jude chuckle. "I'm sure." She picked out a black, silk blouse and khaki trousers.

"You don't look like the I-believe-in-ghosts kind of girl." Nola bent and selected the wedge heels that matched Jude's outfit.

"I'm afraid not. I'm logical, steadfast, and immune to levity." Jude stilled, her mind categorizing the adjectives she'd chosen to describe herself. She was officially, a *spinster*. Either that, or a golden retriever...or a civil war General, depending on how one viewed it.

Defeat permeated every muscle in her body, and she sank to the floor right in front of her closet.

"Ms. Duffy? Are you okay?" Nola sat cross-legged next to her.

A thirty-eight-year-old, boring, virgin, spinster. Alone, for the rest of her life.

"I've never even experienced an orgasm," Jude whispered. "I've been so busy with my work, I never had time."

Nola coughed. "That might be a little more info than I was looking for, but, okay. Get it all out." She rubbed Jude's back.

Her tears fell, and the anguish of a life of

loneliness poured over her like molten lava. She didn't want to be alone. She'd been alone her whole life.

"That's it, Doc. Just get it out, then we'll start anew."

"I don't want to start *anew*! I want a do-over!" Jude flopped back on the floor, executing what she imagined was the proper technique for a midlife temper tantrum. She'd never had one. She'd always been so composed. "I want to go back and be wild and impetuous and…and promiscuous!"

"That a girl. Reach deep."

"I want to *not* meet my deadlines, and use my eating utensils without cleaning them first. I want to run barefoot outside and risk fungal infections. I want to use profanity!"

"Let's hear it!"

Jude looked at her Fairy Godmaid and settled her teeth on her bottom lip. "F-f-f…" She shook her head. "I can't do it. That's too vulgar."

"Okay, let's start small. How about…" Nola's lips twisted. "Son of a bitch."

A smile curved the edges of Jude's lips. "Evan Maddox is a son of a bitch!" She expelled a huge sigh. "God, that felt good." She frowned. "But so disdainfully shallow."

"We need to bottom out before we can rebuild," Nola cooed.

Jude's hopelessness rekindled. "I'm afraid I'm…un-rebuildable." She sniffled and rolled onto her side, a fetal position for ruminating. "I'm doomed to be alone forever."

A *new* Jude? Ridiculous, but she did have dreams and she did have needs; ones she'd never allowed herself to ponder upon for fear of being…selfish…non-benevolent…imperiously self-involved like so many of her peers.

Like her parents and then Evan, when they'd abandoned her over and over again in pursuit of their own dreams.

Could she be different? Could there be a happy medium? Had she given up reaching for the things she wanted from life, as penance over some misconstrued sense of unworthiness?

She flipped to her stomach and propped herself on her elbows. "Reinvention brings conflict. Conflict is disconcerting to me."

"Aw, honey. A little conflict is good for the soul. It lets us know what we're made of."

She rested her face in her palms. "I should

be content with my life."

Nola frowned. "Content? That sounds like the thoughts of an abandon dog at the pound. You deserve more." She smiled that impish smile. "What do you *want*, Jude Duffy?"

Jude rested her chin on the backs of her hands. Lying on any floor was emphatically disgusting. She hardly recognized herself. Maybe that was a good thing because, so far, being Dr. Jude Duffy had yielded very little happiness.

"A child." Someone to love, a family. She'd never been part of a real family. She wanted one of her own. "I've published a few children's books between my journal publications."

Fairy Godmother became silent for a moment. "Wow. I was really hoping for easy. Like a new job or a better haircut or something." Nola stood, grabbed Jude's hand and pulled her to her unsteady feet. "But we can work with that. You're at Castle Alainn in the most mystical month of the year. October is when the ghosts of the *Tragic Lovers* haunt, looking for star-crossed lovers to unite. What about a nice man to date?"

Jude slumped. "Yes, I suppose I'm asking for too much." She didn't really *want* a man. They were...recalcitrant at best and had never brought her happiness. She just wanted the baby one could provide.

"What about adoption?"

Jude shook her head. Her co-worker had waited seven years for her adoption to become final. "I'm too old to wait for the paperwork to go through."

"Artificial insemination?"

She grimaced. "One doesn't really know whose genes are in that tube. I'd like to at least know something about my child's father's genetics. Only…" She turned her back on Nola and rummaged through her shoe selection for the week.

"What?" Nola encouraged.

Jude sighed and turned to her confidant. "I've only had one man interested in me my whole life. And he was gay. Those are not promising statistics."

"Statistics shouldn't be applied to love." Nola rested her hands on her slim hips. "Let's start with having a little fun getting to know the new Ms. Duffy. Now get dressed and be down in the lobby in thirty minutes. I have a feeling your life is about to get interesting."

Nola closed Jude's suitcase and stowed it in

the closet. She walked toward the suite door, then turned back with a smile. "One never knows when one's destiny will be fulfilled."

She winked and left Jude to her own thoughts...and her *hair*.

Who the heck "one" was, Jude had no idea. Certainly not her.

She flicked on the TV to some talk show. She never watched TV and this ridiculousness was exactly why.

Her stomach heaved as she recognized Evan and Timothy on *USA Buzz*, introducing their new reality show and the surrogate who would deliver their love child. Jude had made them famous.

She dropped to the bed and stared at the screen.

"Our little bundle of joy is due in May!"

Jude flinched at Evan's words. He'd wanted to wait to have sex, to have a family. How ironic is it that his new lover had achieved all she'd ever wanted, without even having the right parts.

A steel knife jabbed her windpipe, her heart fractured in two. Was she destined to be alone forever? Or could Nola be right?

Not that she didn't like herself, but there

was certainly room for improvement. She was a product of her upbringing—afraid to live on the edge, frightened of any loss of control. But where had that gotten her?

Jude fell back on the bed, a disreputable thought squeezing through her mind. She was thirty-eight with only one superficial relationship behind her. Her chance of securing another relationship before her eggs dried up, was close to non-existent. Desperate times called for desperate measures.

She lifted her head just in time to see the sonogram of Evan's child as he lay protected in the surrogate's womb.

Could she do it?

She dropped her head and stared at the ceiling a second time. The Gigolo Beast. Now *there* were some impressive, non-committal genetics. Genetics that didn't necessarily have to be attracted to her. They could be paid for. No messy emotions, no regrets.

Jude rolled to the side onto her elbow and dug through the welcome basket on her nightstand for a directory of services. Chocolates, hand cream, Vitamin B, an ice pack, a banana... Hangover cures? How strange. And a romance novel...*Flirting With Sin* by Naima

Simone.

Sin...how apropos. This Simone chick was eerily psychic.

Jude glanced toward the mirror on the wall. Yes, she was flirting with sin, but she had no choice. She squinted to blur her reflection. She had potential, but more importantly, she had an understanding of the male psyche, and the workings of the human species' innate need to procreate.

Yes, she'd have to work with her strengths. She sighed, as an errant curl sprang from what was left of her chignon. And hide her weaknesses.

Goodbye, staid, stuffy, Duffy.

Hello, sinner.

Four

"The devil has put a penalty on all things we enjoy in life. Either we suffer in health or we suffer in soul or we get fat."
Albert Einstein

Thirty minutes later, Jude entered the lobby of Castle Alainn, secretly tugging at the seat of her too-tight trousers. She took a deep breath to settle her pounding pulse and reached for the comfort of the Almond Joy in her pocket.

She was a household joke. The people bustling around the lobby possibly knew of her pitiful circumstances, her miscalculations, her naivety in the face of relationships.

She was a casualty in the war of love.

"Hello there."

A nasally, masculine voice pulled her from her tugging and self-degradation, and she looked up to find a hulking man standing before her. His neck had the girth of a much larger man, but he was only about five-foot-ten. Short and stocky with an expensive haircut and hardened features. And tan...he was quite tan. He wasn't homely, but rather handsome, in a bronzed, professional wrestler type of way.

"Hello," she managed. Men didn't usually seek her out.

His gaze traversed her bosom first, then her face, then her French twist, which had taken twenty-nine of the thirty minutes she'd used to get ready. His smirk and shifty eyes were a bit disconcerting.

"I'm Richard Fantome, heir to Fantome Fitness." He held out his beefy hand and she stared at it. She released the strap of her Monili Lambskin backpack and placed her hand in his.

His grip was strong and sweaty. "Nice to meet you, Jude Du..." Had he seen last night's broadcast of the *Spawn of Satan's* show? "Darling. Jude Darling."

An unnaturally white, toothy smile covered half his tawny face.

"I saw you last night at the bar. I noticed your interest in me." He kissed her hand.

Her brows shot up. Oh, how entertaining. A narcissist. "I'm sorry, but I didn't notice you."

He frowned, as she expected. "Well, I'll have to fix that, then. The castle tour? Unless, of course, you'd rather we went our own way."

Jude smiled as Mr. Fantome glanced in the mirror behind the lobby desk, straightened his hair, and flexed.

"That sounds intriguing." She wrinkled her nose. "But I'm quite interested in the castle tour, thank you."

"That's acceptable." He crowded her into a corner of the room until she was backed against the stone wall. "We'll have plenty of time to get acquainted." One of his brows lifted and the other lowered in a dastardly, Snidely Whiplash effect.

Mr. Fantome placed one hand on the wall next to her head. "Are you interested in fitness, sweetheart?" His bicep contracted in her peripheral vision, bulging under his tight V-neck sweater. He moved closer and whispered in her ear. "I bench four-twenty-five." His breath smelled of Listerine. "I bet I could bench you."

Jude jolted in revelation. This man wanted her? Anthropologically speaking, she wasn't the most attractive woman in the room. But considering her bosom and hip width, perhaps Mr. Fantome was subconsciously attracted to her reproductive attributes.

Reproductive…

This could be an advantageous pairing, after all…in a self-sacrificing aspect, considering Mr. Fantome's overly tight jeans, constrictive sweater and notoriously large ego.

Jude processed his body language—confident, aggressive… Aggressive would not bode well for her mission. She would need to rectify the situation and ensure control if she were to whip Mr. Fantome into shape for her plans.

Movement caught the corner of her eye, and she glanced past the testosterone filled giant in front of her as The Count approached with a scowl. Her heart rate increased.

She slid from under Mr. Fantome's hulking figure and impulsively grabbed The Count's Carhartt jacket by the collar to peck his cheek. "Brother, dear, you're late again!"

Jude looked at her "brother" with pleading eyes, hoping he would follow her lead and instill in the Hulk's mind, that she had a protector if need be.

The Count lifted his gaze from hers to the man lurking behind her. His lips twitched just before they came down on hers with a vengeance, devouring her surprised gasp with his mouth and tongue and doing other unfamiliar naughty things.

The kiss was…*magnificent*.

The way he consumed her, tasted her, demolished all her senses until she couldn't think straight. *Paid escort.*

His hand reached around, and he palmed her bottom. Her eyes popped open, and a squeak escaped, as she pulled back from him in shock.

"Brother, my ass. I've been looking all over for you, Pumpkin." He glanced at his watch. "We have just enough time for that quickie before lunch."

She lifted her gaze to his mocking one. The Beast, Vlad the Impaler, Count Dangerous…whatever she decided he would be today. Those haunting eyes were dark last night. Today, they were an amber storm. She was mesmerized. Absolutely spellbound by his darkness…and his double-crossing treachery.

He grabbed her arm and dragged her toward

an adjacent hallway near the center staircase. She quickly regained her bearings and yanked her arm from his tight grasp. Meeting him eye for eye, she remained fixed on the lethal whiskey daggers in his gaze.

"Don't you remember all those naughty things you said you'd do to me last night, darling?" His smirk was malevolent. She squinted, looking for the points of his incisors to protrude from his succulent lips. Yes, today he would be Dracula, King of the Damned.

"What, like shoot you with wooden bullets to put you out of your misery?"

The Hulk chose that moment to mark his territory. "Excuse me, but Miss Darling and I are going on the castle tour together." His nostrils flared in warning. "She's been matched with me as a contest winner this month."

Drac's hypnotic gaze stayed riveted to hers. "Ms. *Darling*," he drawled the 'l' like he was licking rich chocolate ice cream from a cone, "has already consented to a very personal tour with me."

Hulk smirked. "She obviously gets around."

Drac's fist tunneled past Jude's ear like a 747 through a jet stream. It struck the Hulk's chin with a wrenching crack, the punch faster than any body movement she'd ever witnessed.

The violence sent a shudder down her spine, and she glanced at the titanic brute on the floor.

The scar down the side of The Count's face throbbed, his jaw clenched, and those amber eyes had turned dark and macabre. He spun and pulled her to a dark corridor behind the lobby. She stumbled behind him as he lifted a thick tapestry that hung the length of one wall to expose a secret wooden door. He opened the door and tugged her through to a stairwell.

They quickly descended to a gloomy, dank hallway below the castle. *His lair.*

He stopped once the door at the top of the stairs snapped closed and swatted her behind.

"Ouch!" She rubbed her offended bottom. "What on Earth?"

He held out half an Almond Joy wrapper. "*This* was stuck on your ass, Ms. Darling."

Jude's cheeks heated, even in the cold, inky, stone-lined hallway.

Okay, so shedding Stuffy Duffy wasn't going to be so easy, after all.

Five

"When you are courting a nice girl, an hour seems like a second. When you sit on a red-hot cinder, a second seems like an hour. That's relativity."
Albert Einstein

For Christ's sake, the woman was pure substantiated sin.

Those voluptuous curves tucked into clothes that made Beck wonder about the rises and hollows he'd kill to explore. Those mountainous, pert breasts. The sensually hard nipples poking provocatively through her thin shirt. The perky ass that twitched when she walked, and those long legs…

All that creamy skin begged to be touched and marked. Her incredible copper hair waited to be unleashed.

Beck wanted to strip her bare and mess her The. Fuck. Up. He wanted to run his hands over her soft, soft, flesh and play in those silky, copper curls until they were tangled around his body, holding him while he stroked inside her 'til she came.

She was nutty, erratic…deranged. For God's sake, she drank like a fish, talked to herself and had convinced herself to marry a gay guy.

God, he was hard again. She was a temptation he wanted to corrupt. One he should run from. If she found out who he was, what he'd done to her…

He pulled harder on her hand and paced faster down the secret hallway running the length of the west wing.

If she wanted a tour, he'd give her a damn tour. "I can't believe a woman of your intelligence would be attracted to that."

She stopped in her tracks and his hand slipped from hers. "What do you think you're doing? This is kidnapping. Are you planning on having your way with me? Raping me in the bowels of your dungeon?" She adjusted her ridiculous hair, ramming the dislodged strands back into the straight jacket of a bun he wanted to rip apart.

He pressed his finger and thumb into his eye sockets. This was not in his plan for redemption. Messing with fire would only get him burned.

"No, I'm not going to rape you. I'm saving you from that asshole." Why, he didn't know. Or maybe he did. Penance? He only knew he'd sensed every move she'd made since her arrival.

And he didn't like it. It was creepy and unacceptable.

Christ, what was wrong with him? He dropped his hand. Had he gone too long without sex?

"He was harmless. A prime specimen of narcissistic personality disorder. All you had to do was play along, and then go on your way." She drew an alcohol wipe from her bag, tore it open and cleansed her hands. "Why would you even care whom I cavort with. I'm a grown, single woman. I can be with whomever I want."

Beck grabbed the offending thing and threw it to the ground. "Stop doing that. You're going to get chapped." He knew her. Somewhere deep in his soul. And it sucked.

"I'm preventing illness."

"Let your damn immune system strengthen itself by exposing yourself to a few germs once in a while."

The woman frowned. Those pale green eyes bore into him like alien x-ray vision. "I was often sick as a child. I suppose a hardy immortal like you doesn't ever worry about getting sick. You probably relish the thought of swapping germs."

Those full lips pouted adorably. He didn't need adorable right now. And he also needed less of that magnificent rack being lifted as she crossed her arms underneath her breasts.

Her hair followed the sexual assault and rebelliously burst free from its iron hold at the back of her head. Those fiery curls tumbling past her shoulders were his undoing. That, and the fact she inhaled sharply in surprise and ran her tongue nervously over her plush bottom lip, which drove him fucking nuts.

"As a matter of fact, I do enjoy swapping germs. Right now, all I want to do is take that smart mouth of yours with mine and shove my tongue so far inside I get to lick and taste every part. I want to share every germ and fill you with everything I have."

"You do?" Those gorgeous, green eyes widened and her hands dropped to her sides. "I-I mean, you wouldn't dare."

He smiled. "You shouldn't have said that."

Beck grabbed her hands and pinned them against the stone wall next to her head, trapping her with his body. He stared into her eyes for a fraction of a second, deciding, fighting a primal urge to dominate this sassy, forbidden woman.

He had no idea what the fuck had come over him since she'd arrived at the castle.

And right now, he didn't care.

He lashed out with his tongue and tasted that pouty, lower lip. It was soft...and oh, so sweet.

She sighed as her head dropped back against the wall, eyes closed.

"You like that," he taunted the little witch.

"I...I'm not sure." She opened one eye. "We might have to try it again. I don't have much experience."

Oh yes, she was a sorceress.

He growled, then took her mouth with a yearning he hadn't felt in years. He'd teach her a lesson about being...being...so fucking enchanting.

But it was she, in all her unconstrained innocence, that taught him. She pressed her 1940's pin-up body against him and took charge of the kiss, nipping and nibbling his lips, sucking like he was a goddamn lollipop. What could she do with that mouth on his cock? He groaned. Her tongue danced and twined with his. Accepting everything he gave, she met him stroke for stroke.

Who knew?

He pressed his erection into her writhing hips. She was a torrid bundle of sensual discovery. A siren wired for sex.

Beck pulled away before he took her right against the wall. He wasn't that guy. Okay, he used to be, but she wasn't that girl. He grabbed her hand and led her down the hallway toward his private room.

Jude stumbled. "Wait, wait." She let go of his hand and bent to massage her ankle.

He grimaced as a lash of guilt swept through him and then lifted her into his arms. Her soft body pressed against his, was going to kill him.

"Put me down. Where are we going?"

"Someplace I can teach you a lesson about the art of restraint."

"I don't want restraint." Indignation sharpened her voice. "I want liberty!"

"Yeah, well I have the feeling Mr. Fit 'N' Tan is not the kind of guy you want liberating you." He caught her knowing smirk in his peripheral vision. "And neither am I."

He approached his suite door and placed her gently on her feet. She glanced down at his earnest erection, then lifted her eyes to his.

"Ignore that." He turned the key and then scooped her back into his arms, entering his lair.

Six

"Any man who can drive safely while kissing a pretty girl, is simply not giving the kiss the attention it deserves."
Albert Einstein

He'd hit him. He'd belted the poor, dumb bruiser like it had meant nothing at all.

Except it did to her.

Nobody had ever stood up for her. She'd always had to stand up for herself.

Beast shed his Carhartt jacket, exposing an exquisitely sculpted body beneath a faded LA Dodgers T-shirt and a pair of jeans. Hard muscle flexed across his large shoulders as he arranged logs in the fireplace. The room was small, cold, and simplistic in function. Nothing like the luxurious rooms upstairs. A large bed, two, what looked to be nineteenth century leather rockers, and an end table. A beautiful, rustic wooden table sat in the center of the room, supported by twisted, gnarled tree limbs. It was provocative and beautiful, just like its owner.

She shivered as he worked in complete silence. "That table is beautiful. Where did you get it? The patterns of the rings are stunning."

"I made it."

She jolted. He was an enigma. A talented, handsome, mysterious libertine. "I don't even know your name."

He flinched.

"I can't keep calling you Beast and Count. It's rather presumptuous."

He glanced over his shoulder, those golden eyes piercing her. "You'd be smart to keep considering me a monster. I'm not a good bet for whatever you're up to."

Her lips twisted. Did he know what she had planned? "I don't know what you're talking about."

He stood, his eyes traversing her body as she sat on the bed, filling with interest as his gaze stilled on her bosom. She glanced down, expecting to find her clothes had surreptitiously fallen off.

His eyes returned to hers. "I get the feeling you are up to no good. And, for some reason, I keep ending up in the position to set you straight."

"You had no reason to 'set me straight' today. I had complete control of the situation."

The Beast's brows lowered. "Like last night when you propositioned me?"

Her heart clenched and her spine tightened. Did she? Oh God, she didn't remember. "I-I assumed that was what you were interested in when you approached me."

He shook his head and his beautiful lips lifted at the corners. "I don't make a habit of taking advantage of drunk, distressed women."

"I'm not distressed," she lied. "I may have been a tad bit intoxicated, but I'm hardly distressed."

The Beast laughed. It was a stunning sight. She couldn't help but search out those canines just to be sure. Things in this castle all seemed so…strange.

"Honey, you make a nun during Catholic school detention look like she's channeling Richard Simmons."

She shot him a sneer, then stared down at

her hands. Her ankle throbbed, but she couldn't help the smile that crept over her lips. Her Beast had studied her well.

He sat next to her on the bed, the heat from his body warming her.

"Beckette. My name is Beckette." He lifted her ankle onto his lap, removed her shoe, and ran his hand over the minor swelling that had started. "I'm sorry I hurt you. I'm a bastard and tend to hurt people when they get close. It's my curse. That's why I don't do emotional attachments." He smirked. "As if I were even capable."

Like finding two almonds in a bite-size Almond Joy, her future flashed brightly in her mind. Yes, he'd be *the one*.

Her heart beat wildly as she reviewed the ramifications of what she wanted to do…seduce him. Seduce Beckette, The Beast, the man of mystery and beauty. She wanted this emotionally stunted, beautiful man to be the one to take her virginity, father her child…without him knowing, of course. She didn't need a man. Not that he'd want her. He was a perfect stranger, never to be thought of again.

She was ovulating. She'd always had her menses schedule plotted in her brain. Now all she had to do was get him to take her to bed.

It was ludicrous. It was unethical. But she was desperate.

Our little bundle of joy will be arriving in May!

She pulled her foot from The Count's lap, then stood and slid off her other shoe. She paced the small room without a limp. Her nerves had numbed the pain. He watched her, humor lighting his secretive eyes. This man was dangerous, hardened, disreputable. Perfect for an unscrupulous mission.

But he was also smart. She needed to include that in her calculations.

"I'm fine, really." She stood with her back to him and covertly unbuttoned the top of her blouse. Cleavage. Men liked cleavage. She turned and tried to swing her hair in the sultry way women did. Her head thudded against a gourd lantern hanging from a shelf.

Smooth.

He leaned back on his hands and smirked, his eyes zeroing in on her burgeoning breasts. She had a good bosom, she'd been told. It'd be advantageous to use her positive attributes to the best of her ability.

She noted his body language—visual interest, pulsating carotid in the neck, relaxed posture, erection.

All promising signs.

* * * *

Beck almost came in his jeans, right then and there. "Yes, you are."

What was this naive, little tabby cat up to? Parading around his fucking bedroom like some vixen in heat.

She placed her hand just above that magnificent rack and took a deep breath. "Okay, how do we do this? Do I pay you first?"

He practically choked. Was she serious? Beck examined her flawless face. Yeah, she was serious…and nervous as hell. "Depends on what you're looking for, sweetheart."

Jude paced back and forth in front of him, driving him nuts with the wiggle in her hips. "Sex. I'd like to have sex with you." She faced him, her eyes wide and pleading, then held her palm in the air, facing him. "Nothing crazy. Just plain missionary would be acceptable. Do you have a current health history on hand?" Her little ass twitched as she rushed to her huge backpack and dumped it on his bed.

The woman had everything to survive the apocalypse. She grabbed a banded file the size of an envelope then whipped out a piece of paper. She held it toward him in her trembling hand. "Here's mine. I always carry it."

Beck just stared. The woman was certifiable.

And fucking innocently sexy as all hell.

He didn't do innocent, but this game was an amusing distraction from his frustrations. He leaned forward and rested his elbows on his knees as she stood there with that damn health history.

"Do you like to be tied up, Jude?" he whispered.

Her eyes widened.

"Because I charge more for bondage, and threesomes are definitely out. I only work one-on-one. If you'd like to incorporate sex toys, it will be an extra fifty a night. Seventy-five if I have to provide batteries."

The paper drifted from her stiff hand and floated to the floor at his feet. Her sensuous lips parted. Her quick intake of her breath and the way her breasts rose did nothing to calm his libido. He almost felt guilty for toying with her.

She didn't respond, so he tweaked a little

harder, relishing this small window of joy to brighten his dark existence. "Now, role-playing is a whole other price list. Depending on the cost of the costumes and props, it could run you into the thousands. I do a great dominating circus clown." He pulled his T-shirt over his head.

The woman's gaze caressed his chest as he waited for her response. "Fine, I'm in a generous mood. I'll do you a quickie for thirty-five bucks. Lose the panties." He stood and walked toward her. He didn't know how far he'd actually take this, but he was having too much fun to stop now.

When he got close enough, she ran one of her soft hands down the center of his chest, exploring him in a slow descent, making every nerve in his body burn with a yearning and desire he'd never felt.

The witch's touch blew his mind.

Sex had always been just a physical release to him. A way to forget the pain.

But this was…different.

He inhaled sharply as her little hands mapped his form. It was as if she'd never seen a half-naked man before. Christ, she'd almost been married. She had to have seen one.

"Can you do a Russian accent with that circus clown?"

Beck slowly tilted his head. *"Da, Ljubimaja moja." Yes, my sweetheart.*

Her mouth formed an 'O.' She stepped back and fastidiously undid each button on her shirt. Once she'd exposed all that beautiful skin sprinkled with golden freckles and the pink, lacy bra lovingly holding those gorgeous breasts, she lifted her eyes to his. "Okay, let's proceed. Do you need a deposit up front? Where do you want me to lie down?"

Jesus H. Christ. She was going to be the death of him. Like she was asking to get her oil changed. But Miss Duffy was always tense and, God help him, he couldn't stop from reaching out to stroke the velvet, freckled skin on her shoulder. Couldn't refrain from touching his lips to her pale skin for a small taste. He was fascinated by this shy, nervous version of her. She was like a drug to him, calling out, luring him in, placing a spell on him.

He bent his head and kissed the side of her neck. Soft, silky, and the smell... He couldn't get enough. Clean, fresh and spicy. Like lavender. The same scent he'd noticed in her room.

He was done.

She sighed and dropped her head back. That's all Beck needed. He slid her blouse off her shoulders, touching as much of her as possible. He herded her toward the bed. As the backs of her knees hit, she fell back and he followed her down. The woman was temptation. For Christ's sake, he'd been celibate for a fucking year...never even tempted. Why now?

He had to taste that mouth again. His lips touched hers and, as his tongue found its way inside, an arctic chill skirted his back. It was the most pleasurable sensation. Her nipples beaded beneath the soft satin of her bra, teasing his bare chest, and she moaned.

The kiss was... inspiring.

Beck hadn't planned on making love to this quirky woman. But he couldn't resist her siren's call. He had no control as he ran his palm down her chest and finally glided his fingers over her incredible breasts.

"What I want to do to you," he whispered against her lips, "is probably outlawed in over forty states."

She wriggled underneath him, making his erection throb. He pulled her hands above her head and pinned them to the bed. Her eyes snapped open. She blushed from head to toe, her breasts thrust forward. It was the most beautiful thing he'd ever seen, but he knew women. She may want him, but this hellion was scared shitless.

He rolled off of her to his back and pulled her close. "What's wrong, Jude?"

The Doc took a deep breath. "Could we possibly take things just a bit slower? I mean, I'm thoroughly aroused, it's just…"

Beck couldn't help the laugh that escaped him. This woman was some piece of work. "Aroused? I'm thrilled I could *arouse* you."

"Well, it is your job, isn't it? I'm sure you've had training, considering…"

Humored by her naiveté, Beck smiled and looked into a face that had somehow become familiar to him. In only twenty-four hours? Sobriety was making him crazy. Was she kidding?

Nope, those big eyes and the way her white teeth worried her full bottom lip, said she was shit-ass serious.

"Jude…" What could he say? He didn't want her to know who he really was. He kept to himself, had altered his appearance. His hair was longer, his face a bit fuller, all to remain anonymous during his recovery. If she found out who he was, she was smart enough to make the connection to his past, to what he'd done to her and her parents. He needed to discourage her 'cause, God knew, *he* wasn't going to be strong enough to resist her. And, like all the others, he'd end up disappointing her, hurting her, if she got too close.

He stood, then glanced at his watch. "Honey, my next appointment is about to arrive. So unless you're interested in the four hundred bucks it'll cost you to watch, you'd better start undressing so we can get to business."

The Doc's mouth dropped open as she sat up on the bed, her shirt falling down her arms to further expose the temptation that was only Jude Duffy. She had no idea…

She hugged her shirt to her chest. "I-I…" Good. His plan to scare her away was working. "Do you take credit cards? I'm afraid I don't use cash often, considering the bonuses one can retrieve from current credit card programs."

For Christ's sake.

A knock echoed through the room, and he kept his eyes on her as he cracked the door.

"Yeah?"

"I'm a bit knackered, boyo." Ennis swayed on his feet. "I need a kip before I do any manual labor. See you in a few hours."

"Fine. Go sleep then I'll meet you at six." Beck shut the door and turned toward Jude.

She stood and briskly walked to where she'd dumped her purse. "Should we continue with our arrangement then?" She opened her wallet and handed him her credit card.

He was going straight to hell. "Honey, you seem a bit nervous. What if I said this next hour was on the house and we just hung out and talked? Maybe we'll grab a pizza downtown? I'm a little hungry."

Talking was the last thing he wanted to do, but he was no good for her and thanks to AA he knew where to draw his boundaries. After today, he'd hopefully never see her again.

She smiled and the sight stole his breath from his lungs. "I'd like that very much." She buttoned her blouse and sat on the bed, her back ramrod straight, little bare feet crossed and her virtuous pleasure shining through.

He put his T-shirt back on and cursed himself for being so damn noble. He'd never been noble before. Why now?

Must be the sobriety.

They walked the short distance downtown and found a cozy checkered table at Guido's Pizza. His little tabby cat chattered about her research, her rock star, asshole parents who'd ignored her, and the guy who'd left her for another man.

About the tragic death of her parents, the first innocent souls he'd murdered, and how they'd given away her inheritance. And about the mysterious trust fund from an anonymous benefactor who'd supported her education.

Remorse fermented in his chest, as it always did. But, through her melodic chitchat, he allowed himself a few moments of peace. A peace that didn't include alcohol.

There was something about her. Something he had no right exploring.

"This was lovely." She stood, leaving him cold and empty. "You were worth every penny." She winked, then shoved her arms into her tweed blazer.

"I was free."

"Precisely." Jude opened a small book and fished a pen from her bag. "I'm open tomorrow evening at nine p.m." She glanced at him. "Will that do to complete our transaction?"

Son of a bitch. She couldn't be serious. He needed to go on the offensive and end this little game before things got out of hand. Before he got too close and caused her inevitable pain. "Why are you so hell bent on having sex? Rebound situations are never healthy. There is the distinct possibility of post-traumatic stress disorder."

She wrote in her book as though she hadn't heard a word he'd said. "Hogwash. And don't joke about PTSD, Mr.…." Her brows furrowed. "You didn't tell me your last name. I'll need your last name so I can reference your health history. I have access to most medical databases."

He wasn't just going to hell. He was *in* hell. "You're not looking up my private information. I'm as clean as a whistle."

She slammed her book shut and sighed. "Fine. We can go over whatever records you can provide tomorrow night. I'd like just the missionary position, no lights. I'll pencil you in from nine to nine fifteen."

"Why do I feel so used?"

Her brows rose. "Because, Mr. Beckette, I need to lose my virginity and you're just the man to do it."

Seven

*"If we knew what it was we were doing,
it would not be called research, would it"?
Albert Einstein*

Oh, this was going to work out superbly. Jude glanced at the selection of condoms in the adult entertainment store. Not that she needed a condom for what she had planned. She needed a condom with small puncture holes.

She took a deep breath. This was the most diabolical, underhanded, frivolous thing she'd ever done. But she'd only ever wanted one thing in her life and this was the only way to get it.

If she logically reasoned with herself, there would be no harm. A man like Mr. Beckette would want no part of a child with his active, gigolo lifestyle. So keeping her pregnancy secret after all was said and done, would be a win-win for both parties.

It was her emotional reasoning that kept interfering with her mission.

He was a man of mystery—dark, brooding, bossy. Yet, he'd taken such great care with her, noticing how nervous she was, switching gears on her. No one noticed anything about Jude. Ever. Thank goodness, because the Jude Duffy who had shown up for this week's vacation at Castle Alainn was like no Jude Duffy she knew. Her conduct was erratic, her thoughts preposterous, and her inclinations toward wayward behavior, uncontrollable.

It was a curse…or perhaps a spell of some sort. This was October, after all.

Dotted, ribbed, studded. Ultra thin, Tantric… For goodness sake, this was worse than selecting a feminine hygiene product. She was a top-notch scientist and didn't go into any unknown situation without researching thoroughly.

She grabbed the closest box and tossed it into her basket. She ambled down the aisle and grabbed the "Majik Mike," a seven-function, dual-action vaginal vibrator with ball bearings.

My… She shook her head then added it to

her other purchases.

She reached the checkout counter and unloaded her basket in front of the tattooed girl manning the register.

"Oh, you'll love this vibrator. Here, let me put batteries in so we can make sure it works. I'll show you all the options."

Jude smiled. If only the help at her local health food store was as enthusiastic. The girl nimbly opened the package and inserted the small batteries. Once she'd finished, she held up the vibrator and flicked a switch. "This is the power button. Hear how quiet it is? It's awesome...feel." The girl held the vibrator to Jude's cheek.

Ohhh... Jude lifted her hand to hold it closer.

"And if we turn this switch, we get a pulsating vibration." The girl turned a small ring around the base of the vibrator and an intriguing, undulating pressure began against Jude's cheek. "Gets me to orgasm every time."

Jude stroked the vibrator down her arm. "Oh, I like that! You do realize an orgasm is not just intended for pleasure? The biological function is to help move the sperm toward the uterus. It's a necessity."

The pierced girl shrugged. "Depends on what you want out of the hook-up—sex or pregnancy."

Jude smiled. "Oh, I'm looking for impregnation. An orgasm would only be an added perk. Are there different cadence options available on the 'Majik Mike?' I should condition my muscles to produce an orgasm."

"What the *hell* do you think you're doing?"

Jude flinched. Beckette, The Beast.

She turned as she tucked the buzzing vibrator behind her back. "Mr. Beckette. Hello."

The whirring continued no matter how hard she held it. She fumbled blindly for the power switch, but couldn't find it. "I was shopping for…"

His lips thinned. His body crowded her as he reached behind her and grabbed the vibrator. Of course, a professional like him would know exactly where the power button was, and he adroitly turned it off and slammed it on the counter. "You won't be needing that."

He had the audacity to move her out of the way. "Or this, or this, or this…" He tossed her pornographic magazines, feminine wash and, finally, her Marvin Gaye CD toward the cashier. The Beasts eyes lifted. "And you definitely don't need this." He shoved *The Art of Orgasm, How To Get Your Lover to Understand The G-Spot* video clear across checkout.

You deserve more. Nola's words rang in her head. No paid gigolo was going to tell her how their encounter was going to go. She was the customer and the customer was *always* right.

The Beast tossed the edible panties back into her basket. "These you can keep."

Her blood boiled. She jumped up and leaned over the counter, backside in the air, and reached beside the cashier's feet to collect the items. "I will not be treated like a child. Maybe these aren't for you. Maybe I found someone else. Someone more capable of meeting my needs. Like Mr. Fantome." Jude threw the items over her shoulder and back onto the checkout counter.

"I'm more than you can handle, Baby. You won't be propositioning anyone else." Beck pulled her off the counter by the hips and threw her over his shoulder like she weighed nothing at all. He threw down a twenty, grabbed the edible panties and marched out the door.

Oh, this *was* going to work out superbly.

* * * *

"Beckette?"

Beck looked over his shoulder to find Liam and Alana Fitzgerald approaching down the sidewalk. Liam glanced up at the sign to the goddamned sex shop Jude had been exploring for the sake of *research*.

Beck cringed.

"Hello Liam, Alana. I was just helping Ms. Duffy over this puddle." He kept the witch on his shoulder regardless of her protests. He didn't dare give her a chance to speak. God only knew what would come out of her mouth.

"Miss Duffy needs to get back to the resort and prepare for dinner. Mr. Fantome has requested she be seated with him. And don't you have to check the pipes in Ms. Carmichael's suite?"

Jude stiffened in his arms. Damn the woman and her intelligence. She'd figured him out.

"Put me down this instant!"

Beck dumped her on her feet. She straightened her jacket and tucked her hair back into its pristine predicament. She had a thing for severe and tidy that called to him to mess her up.

She glared at him, her back to the owners of

the resort. "Check the pipes? Is that what we're calling it now?"

The woman really did have a flair for dramatics. He crossed his arms, hiding the edible panties.

"Miss Duffy." Alana tapped Jude's shoulder and she turned to face the meddling matchmaker. "I do hope you're coming to dinner. Mr. Fantome was very taken with you and made special arrangements to dine with you." She winked.

Alana frowned at Beck, shooting him a warning. He was just an employee. Not to be fraternizing with the guests.

"Beckette, the finishing touches also need to be put on the patio pergola for the Monster Ball at the end of the week."

Jude swiveled her head to Beckette. "Mr. Beckette works for you?"

"Yes. He's our maintenance man." Alana smiled like a proud mother. Or a mischievous, manipulative, leprechaun. "Our poor Beckette is a widower, you know. Six years now."

A storm brewed in Jude's eyes. "You… You deceived me!"

The shock of hearing his personal life

spilled like a cheap tabloid story, pissed him off. "Now, Miss Duffy. You came to your conclusions all on your own. I simply went along for the ride."

The hellion's jaw tightened and those sparkly greens shot daggers at him. She grabbed the panties from his hand. They fell out of the box, landed in a puddle, and began to dissolve like cotton candy in the rain. She stared at the disintegrating confection, jaw unhinged as if her dreams were going up in smoke.

She said goodbye to the Fitzgeralds, then turned and stomped away.

Why this woman was so hell bent on losing her virginity was a mystery to him. A mystery he'd uncover, long before she plotted her next hair-brained scheme. He'd ruined her life once. He'd be damned if he let it be ruined anymore.

Eight

"Never do anything against conscience
even if the state demands it."
Albert Einstein

Jude shoved her bag from *Between the Sheets* to the bottom of her closet behind her suitcase. Thank goodness she'd had time to go back and collect her research materials.

A maintenance man. A widower, for Christ's sake. He'd deceived her. She needed a man with no morals, no heart. One she could simply exchange monetary funds with, for the excitement of learning about sex and, as a bonus, a pregnancy he'd never care about. Not some charming, grieving artisan.

"You don't look very thrilled about dinner."

Jude jumped at Nola's mysterious appearance in her room, once again. She shrugged and turned back to her frumpy clothing. "It's not that." She ran her hand over a celery cashmere sweater and sighed. "I had everything planned. He was perfect, but he went and ruined it. Now I need to start over." A smidgen of guilt knotted in her chest, but she pushed it away.

"I'm not sure if I want to hear this." Nola sat on the bed and crossed her legs.

Jude's lips twisted. "I had this plan, you see. A harmless one, if all went well. I was going to sleep with Mr. Beckette, the profligate one, and check off two birds with one stone. I'd finally understand what all the fuss is about regarding sex, and I'd most likely get pregnant, considering my current menstruation schedule." Jude glanced away. The loneliness in her heart pushed a tear from her eye. "I know this is ludicrous, unscrupulous even, but I may never get another opportunity like this. I've always wanted a child. Someone to love and nurture and spend my life with. If this doesn't work out, I'll be alone forever."

"Aw, honey." Nola stood and wrapped her arms around Jude. She pulled back, holding Jude's shoulders. "But tell me. Why *not* Mr. Beckette?"

Jude bent to gather a tidy pair of pumps to match her outfit. She walked toward the bed and laid out her staid, stodgy suit, then stared out the window, defeat permeating her being. "He's real now," she whispered.

"He's always been real, Ms. Duffy."

"He was just an unfeeling playboy before." Jude walked into the adjoining bath. "Nothing but a mindless body I could pay for sex and leave with no further compunction. Now…" She dropped her arms from trying to reassemble her French twist. "Now, he's a real man with a real past and real emotions. He's a widower, for goodness sake. And smart and funny, and I find myself inexplicably emotionally attracted to him." She stared at her pale features. "And I can't have sex and get pregnant when my emotions are involved. I need an emotionless, indifferent specimen."

She touched up her makeup and brushed her teeth as Fantome's taut, tan face popped into her mind. She reentered the main suite to dress. "Someone who doesn't have the power to hurt me."

Nola sat on the bed, eying her. "Believe it or not, I understand your crazy thought pattern here. But don't you want to find love?"

Jude laughed. "Love? For me? Nola, look at me. I'm boring, aging and suffering from a slight case of obsessive-compulsive disorder."

Nola's eyebrows rose.

Jude slumped. "You see what I mean? I fall, they don't, and I get hurt. Love is not, and never has been, in the forecast for me. But a child…" She glanced longingly at her make-believe Fairy Godmaid.

Nola smiled. "Anything is possible, Miss Duffy. You just have to believe in yourself."

Jude did believe in herself…the few times she'd been with Beckette. She didn't even know him but, in the short time they'd been together, she'd felt different. Safe and secure and worthy. Those were all things she'd never had before in any relationship. Except with Aunt Aggie, but that didn't count. She was gone now too.

In all her previous relationships, Jude had been required to prove herself, consistently feeling less, not part of the crowd, as if she were an afterthought. "Well, regardless, there's no harm in a single woman wanting to have sex with a single available man. It is the twenty-first century. Anthropologically speaking, casual sex has been around since the beginning of time. Only since the development of religious organizations and their doctrines to control societies, has sex been looked down upon when not practiced within the confines of a marital situation."

Nola's innocent eyes widened. "But you do want love, don't you?"

Jude sank to the bed as a small tear slipped down her cheek. For all her bravado, she did want love. "Yes. It would be nice. But, statistically speaking, an illicit pregnancy is so much more attainable for me. I have to take what I can get."

* * * *

Beck stood in his room, examining the skin graft scars along the left side of his back and arm. He'd never have any feeling there, which was fine by him. He didn't deserve to feel. He'd been cursed long ago for the transgressions of his youth. The plane crash that had killed a young Jude Duffy's parents, his first flight as a new pilot, was only one sin that would haunt him forever.

Being an angry, rebellious, twenty-one-year-old son of a bitch, he'd been busy partying and screwing the airport manager's daughter. He'd rushed his pre-flight check and they'd encountered problems at ten thousand feet. He'd lived, scarred and burned for life, but his trusting cargo had died, his drunken secret kept hidden behind his guilt all these years.

Sixteen years later, he'd killed his wife with his deadly, heartless curse.

Beck rammed his arms into his shirt and tugged it closed. Regardless of the last year of rehab, he was still cursed, still making bad choices.

Like getting involved with Jude Duffy while misleading her about his identity.

It was selfish. He knew damn well if she realized who he was, she'd run for the hills.

But he wanted her like no other woman before.

Beck grunted. The world was a funny place. Putting Jude and Beck together here, now. But, why?

Fate was an evil bitch.

He could tell himself he wasn't interested. He was a pro at being uninterested. But with her, in this place, he couldn't resist.

She was stern and bossy and crazy. Her offbeat buoyancy and zest for learning was refreshing. It drew him like a bee to honey.

And that body and face. Like an angel from

Heaven, made just for him.

Beck shook his head and pulled on his boots. If he didn't know better, he'd think the ghost stories about the castle were true. Destined lovers brought together by the ghosts of tragic lovers from the past.

Why the hell she chose this week to lose her virginity, under his watch, was a mystery. He straightened his tie. For Christ's sake, it was none of his business. Except for slimy Richard Fantome. He had to be here, sniffing up her skirt. How could Beck step aside and let her be ruined by that asshole?

She had no idea what she was getting herself into.

He owed her, in some strange penitential way. Didn't he?

If anyone was going to ruin her, by damn, it was going to be him…again.

Nine

*"There are two ways to live: you can live as
if nothing is a miracle; you can live as if
everything is a miracle."*
Albert Einstein

Standing in the entryway of the large dining
room, Jude rubbed her palms against her thighs,
compressed in the ecru skirt she'd chosen for
dinner. Castle Alainn truly was magical. The
soaring beamed ceiling supported ornate, crystal
chandeliers. Sparkling light spread throughout
the room like glitter. Second story balconies
gave the atmosphere that true old world feel.

"We have a date."

She flinched and inhaled Beck's familiar
woodsy cologne. Amazing how, when attracted
to a potential mate, the human species could tell
who they were without seeing them, and be

stimulated sexually by their scent. "We no longer have an arrangement, Mr. Beckette. You deceived me and I cannot enter into any contract with a person I do not trust." *And am hopelessly attracted to.*

"I didn't deceive you. You jumped to conclusions all on your own, Sweetheart. Isn't that in your studies somewhere? How, when a person wants something so bad, they see what they want to see?"

Jude sneered at him over her shoulder. She should have never looked. He was impeccable in a charcoal suit, black shirt and black tie. So typically *Phantom of the Opera.* "What I want is no longer any of your concern."

She needed to keep her wits about her. Any further emotional enticement toward this beautiful, dark creature would incite the dissolution of her plans.

She gasped as his cheek brushed hers from behind. His scar branded her, marked her, made every nerve tingle with need to be a soothing balm that tore the shadows from his eyes.

"Jude." His breath was warm, his voice the decadence of thick, rich chocolate. "Everything you do is my concern. There is no reasoning this away. It's too late to avoid our inevitable connection."

She needed to break his spell. She turned and confronted his magnificent face. "Our inevitable connection has no bearing on my choices. Emotional connection is cumbersome, capricious, emotive. I want disconnected sex, which means I don't want you anymore."

His succulent lips tipped up at the corners, one side slightly askew due to the mysterious scar. "There is no such thing."

He leaned in, a mere centimeter away from touching her lips with his, and waited, staring intently into her eyes, reading her mind, delving into all her secret desires. He knew...knew she wanted him with her every breath. Knew she found herself lacking. That she'd want forever and a man like Beckette...whatever...would only want one night. He was a loner, an injured soul harboring his grief. Her plans called for a shallow, unfeeling cyborg.

He placed a scarred hand along her face and touched his cheek to hers. "And Miss Jude Duffy, I want *you*."

He kissed her softly on the neck then turned and left with a flip of his invisible vampire cape.

Jude stood frozen, speechless and tingling.

"Miss Duffy?" She startled at the whiny, high-pitched voice of The Hulk at her shoulder. She turned and plastered on a smile, reaffirming the most pertinent course toward her goal. An emotionless, indifferent, unthinking, idiot. Someone she'd feel no regret over, forget in no time.

"Hello, Mr. Fantome."

"Call me Dick, please. Everyone does." He shot her that too-white smile, in that fake tan face.

"I'm sure." She took the arm he offered and followed him to their table. This was going to be a long, exhausting night, but there were usually many in the face of research and attaining one's goals.

* * * *

Beck took his place on the hidden balcony above the dining room. He pulled out the bench to the baby grand and sat as he tried to calm his nerves. He had a perfect view of the woman he couldn't get out of his mind.

She was a romantic. And he was nothing but a cynical jackass. A self-destructive, heartless asshole who was about to commit yet another selfish act. While he wanted Jude with every breath, what he should do was to stay far away and leave her to her safe, silly little dreams.

Especially since she was trying to save him.

She saw him as a mourning widower who might be hurt by a clandestine affair.

And yet, he was going to fuck it all up by sleeping with the most intriguing, irresistible woman he'd ever met, and then leave before he tore her life apart like he did so many others.

It was his only option. Get in and get out.

Could she handle it? Could he?

He didn't have time to ponder the questions. She'd set her sights on Fantome. A man Beck couldn't trust to be gentle. Beck would give her what she wanted then let her take her newfound knowledge into the future. A safe future. A future without him. And he'd carry the memory of her with him into his lonely abyss.

He placed his hands on the keyboard and got lost in the music that was such a part of his life. He couldn't play in front of other people. Not anymore. He'd refused since Elizabeth had died. Music was a reminder of his how his destructive ways had killed her. It had become a window to his barren soul. But here, in the shadows, he could let the songs take him away without anyone in the dining room knowing whose soul was being bared behind the notes.

* * * *

"So, my current net worth is one point two million." The Hulk was killing her with his garlic breath and the apparent need to lean as close as possible whenever he spoke so he could glance down her blouse. Ignoramus.

"That's wonderful." She sipped at her second Long Island Iced Tea. She was becoming rather fond of the drink. Especially tonight. Alcohol might be the only thing that kept her sane.

Fantome smiled as the waiter arrived and placed a new drink next to Jude's plate. "So, what's your favorite kind of music, Sweet Cheeks. Rap? Maybe Rock and Roll?"

Oh, for God's sake. It was like she was on the speed version of "Teen Jeopardy." "I prefer classical or vintage rock. *Unchained Melody* would be one of my favorites but, I have to say, I have a true affinity for The Beatles. My parents always sang *Hey Jude* to me before bed." She tasted the new drink and glanced at the waiter. "What's this?"

"Sparkling water sent by a secret admirer."

He winked then took his leave.

Thank goodness her cell phone beeped, as The Hulk asked which was her favorite, SpongeBob or Patrick. She had no idea whom he was speaking of so she just smiled and looked at the text.

Did you know when you're frustrated you purse your lips and create the sexiest dimple to the left of your mouth?

Jude inhaled.

And did you realize when you discuss your work your eyes sparkle with mischief and wonder?

Who is this? She texted back. As if she already didn't know.

If your dinner date looks down your shirt one more time I'm going to hit him...again. You've had enough liquor tonight.

Jude glanced around the room. Of course, Mr. Beckette wouldn't be here. He was an employee. But he was watching from somewhere like a ghost in the night.

How did you get my number?

I have my ways.

She smiled. *Stop bothering me. I'm on a date.*

He's not a date, he's a punishment. Is he regaling you with an account of his comic book collection and video game scores?

Jude laughed. *I'm hanging up now.*

Finish your dinner and meet me in my room at ten.

ABSOLUTELY NOT!

Wow, CAPS LOCK. You are in a saucy mood. Perfect for what I have planned. Do you want to know what that is, Ms. Duffy? You're going to tell me what you want. Every intimate detail. Dirty talk? I'll give it to you. You want gentle or to be fucked hard, that's what you'll get. Be naked on my bed in one hour. There are places on your body that need my attention. Places I've fantasized about. Places that make me hard every time I'm near you. It's time you took care of that.

Jude dropped the phone like it had spontaneously combusted. Shit, the sensuality in his voice echoed right through the letters. The man was a villain. A monster. A multifaceted, sexy, irresistible temptation.

Caps lock is not saucy. It indicates rage and anger. Now leave me alone. My date and I are having a wonderful time.

I doubt discussing the attributes of SpongeBob wearing underwear is stimulating conversation. Are you wearing underwear?

"Damn spying waiter," Jude mumbled.

There is something about you… Something that makes me want to…overcome. You've enchanted me, Jude Duffy.

No, no, no. She didn't want to enchant him. She didn't want to be drawn in by his wounded soul. She just wanted sex. Sex and a baby. That's it. If she gave in, she'd fall in love. And he'd get over his lustful infatuation by the end of the week and tear out her heart.

That's a lot of responsibility on me.

Who was she kidding? She was already falling for him. Ridiculous.

She held the phone in the air to be sure he saw her click the power button. "Now, Mr. Fantome, are you currently in a relationship? Have you recently been tested for sexually transmitted diseases?"

What the hell was she saying? The beautiful piano music slowly shifted into *Unchained Melody*. The sensual chords were more drawn out than the popular rendition, the new version eerie and lovely and yearning. That song had the

Count written all over it. Damn the man. Was there anything he couldn't do? Oh yeah, fall in love with her.

She sat captured by the seductive aria until a deep tenor from the man who wanted to *overcome* floated around the rafters.

I've hungered for your touch…

She silently recited the entire song along with him. Words she'd always wished applied to her.

God speed your love to me…

At the conclusion, after her emotions had been ripped, torn and shredded by what would never be, after a fatal burst of God-I-could-love-this-man erupted in her chest, she slammed her fork down and leaned back in her chair. "I'm not feeling well, Mr. Fantome."

"It's Dick."

She smirked. "Yes, it is. Do you mind if we call it a night?" She stood and gathered her belongings, then rushed toward the lobby to escape to her room and regroup.

As she rounded the corner, she bumped directly into her phantom. His scent, emanating from the warmth of his chest, enveloped her in a fog of precocious need.

She stepped back and straightened her blouse, hoping to emotionally distance herself from Beck and his assault on her senses. "I didn't know you were so musically talented."

"It's a gift I don't often share." A rueful smile played across his lips. One that seemed forced. As if he'd shared some clandestine confession.

She understood. Certain activities churned up heart-wrenching pain for those with great loss. How long did one need to suffer? Her eyes locked on his. She was done suffering, done with cowardice. "Do you believe in love, Mr. Beckette?" If he did, would she consider taking a shot at love again?

His head tilted, and he gazed at her as if looking upon a silly, naive child. "For others, maybe."

She ignored the clench of her heart, her courage receding. "Yes, that's what I thought." She needed to protect herself from falling in love with any more emotionally unavailable men. It was time to give up. To focus on her goal and have a child she could love and be loved by.

She tried to maneuver past him, but he caught her around the waist with one arm. The pocket of her suit jacket ripped, and she slipped it off to examine the damage.

He pulled the jacket from her hands. "I'm sorry." She didn't know if he meant for the jacket or for not being what she wanted him to be.

"Beck!"

The Count turned as a tall blonde beauty threw herself into his arms. "Oh, Beck. I've missed you so much and have such great news for you...for us!" She pulled back and eyed Jude. "Who is this? You know our deal, Beck. Don't be breaking it."

"Don't worry about our deal, Ava. I never break my promises."

Whatever "deal" the beautiful woman in the tight-fitting, red sequined dress was referring to, Mr. Beck's promise to keep it, corroborated Jude's knowledge that he was only interested in loveless interludes to soothe his damaged soul.

She could relate. Having a child with someone she could easily fall for with no hope of reciprocation, she'd be sentencing herself to a life of heartache every time she looked at her child.

"I'm no one. Excuse me, please." Jude wriggled

out of Beck's arms, leaving him holding her ruined jacket, and hurried toward the stairs.

The job of mating with simple, disenchanting Mr. Fantome would have to wait for another day.

Ten

"If the facts don't fit the theory,
change the facts."
Albert Einstein

The damp, dank darkness of Beck's room suited his mood. A mood that had plagued him for the past two days, ever since he'd *argued* with Jude about love and then left Ava standing in the lobby with her unanswered questions.

He didn't believe in love. But that wasn't what this was.

Jude wanted sex. She'd stated as much. What was all this crap about love?

Women. Women and castle curses.

Jesus H. Christ. Sure, she was amazing, but Beck didn't deserve amazing. Not after killing her parents, plaguing everyone around him with angst and suffering.

He'd tried to redeem himself by setting up her secret trust account. Angel Wings was another Hail Mary in his search for redemption. But his soul still choked on his guilt.

He lifted his soda to his lips and stared at the Jack Daniels sitting across the room next to his Beretta 9mm. The warm wicked liquid called to him, beckoned him to numb the need he'd come to expect whenever he thought of missing out on love.

A life of happiness.

Jude.

She was light to his dark, heaven to his hell. He needed her to be his salvation, but he refused to bring her down with him if he fell off the wagon and became the heartless man he used to be. He refused to do that to Jude.

They hadn't touched each other since she'd been in his room, but he could think of nothing else. It was ludicrous, eerie. The past two nights, they'd been drawn together by fate and circumstances he didn't understand. A chance meeting on the patio at two in the morning. A mutual urge for an indoor swim at three. It seemed forces beyond their control were pushing them together.

He'd shown her how to use a Dremel to carve gourds into lanterns, how to use curly willow to weave chair seats and how to make the perfect cheesecake—a recipe his mother had taught him before she'd given up on him. They'd played hide and seek in the darkness and Jude had found him every time, and he'd taught her how to swim in the shadows of night in the indoor pool.

They'd become friends over toasted marshmallows, but he wanted more. And more meant he would have to face his demons, take a huge risk and trust himself. Tell her the truth about his role in her parents' deaths. About his disease.

Every day he lived to deflect the memories and the self-loathing. Pushing away everything he might destroy by working himself into an exhausted stupor.

Jude should be one of those things he pushed away.

If he let his failures, his offenses invade his soul, alcohol was his only balm. A destructive one. In the past, he'd immersed himself in the world of acting, of make-believe. A place where he could spend most of his waking hours being someone else, avoiding temptation, the guilt and shame. But acting had been a diversion to replace the alcohol, a busy life to keep him from the emotional ties he would inevitably set on fire if he were to sink into oblivion again.

Jude would only be here a few more days. And, on Saturday night at the Monster Ball—thanks to his agent—he would be unmasked. Camera crews would be there to film a public interview for the new role he was about to accept, and Jude would see him for who he really was.

A liar and the epitome of all she despised—fame, inconsistency and an indifference to love. All things that had taken her parents and her ex-fiancé away from her.

She'd leave him, and she'd be safe.

Eleven

*"You have to learn the rules of the game.
And then you have to play
better than anyone else."*
Albert Einstein

Jude stared at the ceiling. Something had woken her. A bad dream about an Indian girl being shot with an arrow while she rushed to save her love.

Loneliness and sadness enveloped her. The room was too cold, and she was hungry.

She'd never eaten dinner. She'd stayed up late researching her pornographic magazines for information on sexuality and intercourse. She didn't have much time left to seduce Mr. Fantome.

Intercourse didn't seem too difficult. It was the sensuality part she couldn't buy into. The feelings, the arousal, the orgasm. She understood how it happened, she just didn't think her body was capable of *allowing* it to happen.

She thought too much.

She rose from bed and pulled on her robe, hoping to find something to comfort her in the resort's kitchen.

The halls were dark and quiet. She slipped down the stairs to the abandoned lower level and into the dimly lit industrial kitchen. The large, glass-fronted refrigerator boasted a host of treats, but what she always wanted most when she was sad was ice cream. It reminded her of Aunt Aggie and all the times she'd spent with the kind woman after her parents had abandoned her for another tour.

Jude moved toward the large freezer and placed her hand on the handle.

"I see you couldn't sleep, either. Thinking of ways to ruin yourself by plotting the seduction of your next victim?"

She screeched and turned to find Beckette leaning on the other side of the large stainless island, looking rumpled and surprisingly attractive. Her heart stilled at the sight of him. What made a disheveled, alpha male so enticing to the female species? She should research that later.

"You frightened me." Being alone with him was not in her best interest. She'd already fallen so far and, on the heels of her dream, she was vulnerable. But she did need an expert's opinion.

She pulled a list she'd made out of her robe pocket and walled off her heart. "Since you are my friend and not a viable candidate for my research, I'd like your input on something. I've made an itinerary for the evening I have the opportunity to lose my virginity with Mr. Fantome. I don't want to look foolish or unprepared."

Beck's brows lowered. "Heaven forbid." He ripped her notes from her hand and focused on the paper.

Jude recited the agenda in her head.

Nine p.m. Lower lights, close all curtains and lock door.

Nine-oh-four p.m. Undress and slide under covers. Allow Mr. Fantome to undress and prepare birth control.

Nine fifteen p.m. Apply lubricating unguent for ease of penetration.

Nine seventeen p.m. Accept Mr. Fantome's

kiss as start of foreplay, expect fondling.

"Expect fondling?" Beck's voice pulled her from her thoughts, his disdain expertly conveyed through his scrunched features.

"What? Should I not expect that yet? Maybe earlier?"

"Oh, for Christ's sake!" He rubbed his eyes then refocused on her notes as she read over his shoulder.

Nine twenty p.m. Missionary mounting, penetration, thrusting, ejaculation.

Nine twenty-four p.m. Mr. Fantome will recover, offer thanks, dress and leave.

"God, kill me now." Beck tore her itinerary into pieces. "Four minutes of sex? That's all you're expecting?"

She was confused by his fervor. "I've researched this, Beckette. A man's orgasm is controlled by the sympathetic portion of the autonomic nervous system, the increased heart rate, and vasodilation for erection. When the lateral orbitofrontal cortex—our thoughtful, reasoning center—shuts down as it does during intercourse, there is no hope for the weary. A man loses all control. Men want to feel good and they want it as soon as possible. By my calculations, they've got, at most, four minutes until ejaculation."

Beckette ran his hand through his hair. "You are some piece of work, Jude Duffy. This is not how it works. You can't plan sex. And you are not having sex with Mr. Fantome."

Jude's stomach turned. Beckette didn't know the complete debauchery of her plan. How could she consider something so unscrupulous as stealing a man's sperm? Even a man as obtuse as Mr. Fantome.

Because I'm desperate.

"It's certainly none of your business. If you don't want to help, I'll have to…wing it." She'd rather wing it with him, but that would be a disaster.

She focused on the large commercial mixer across the room and envisioned a red-headed little girl sitting next to her, making homemade cookies on a snowy Saturday afternoon. Her hunger for a child much outweighed her guilt, but she needed detached, no-emotions-involved sex with someone with no principles. Beck might be emotionally unavailable, able to rip her heart out, but the man had morals and honor. And she'd never be able to forget him.

Mr. Fantome was the perfect choice. He'd impregnate her then walk away to be forever forgotten, her heart intact. She couldn't let The Count get in her way.

"I'm sure you are quite adequate in carnal affairs, Mr. Beckette. Hopefully, it will be as enjoyable for me with Mr. Fantome. He doesn't seem like the type to…linger…so he will be the perfect one-night stand."

"Is that why you're wandering the halls at two in the morning? Because everything will work out perfect and tidy in your plan? Like your hair and your clothes and your little itinerary?"

Shame heated her cheeks. This man saw too much in her. "No, I just couldn't sleep. I had a bad dream."

Beck shot her an incredulous glare then moved around the island and bumped her out of the way. He opened the freezer and walked in, returning seconds later with his arm wrapped around a large tub. "Cherries Garcia?"

Jude smiled. An unfamiliar warmth spread through her at his intuition and care. "Yes, one of my favorites."

"I know. You mentioned it a while back and

I had the cook order some."

The walls around her heart began to crack and crumble, brick by brick.

He opened a drawer and pulled out two spoons, then pushed the drawer closed with his hip. Beck set down the ice cream then lifted her onto the island. A rush of excitement ran through her as he hopped up next to her as if it took little to no effort.

His focus moved to the left of her mouth, and he smiled. "I love the dimple you get when you do that. When you're thinking about something."

His compliment pulled her from her scientific contemplation. "You know when I'm thinking?"

He nodded and stuck another spoonful of ice cream into her mouth. "And when you're nervous or frustrated or excited about something you've just figured out. Your emotions are written all over your face."

She covered her mouth with her hand. "I'm sorry."

"Don't be sorry. I like it. You're honest."

Honest. And here she was, planning to secretly impregnate herself. "How come I don't know anything about you? You're like the spooky mystery of the castle. No one sees you or knows anything about you."

His mouth curved on one end in a wry smile. "There isn't much one would enjoy knowing. I'm not the man you think I am."

"I'm an expert in the human species, Beckette. I'm quite sure I know a little something about the man you are inside, if my research and observation skills are as good as my PhD say they are. Try me."

He glowered as if to scare her away then jumped off the counter and stood between her knees. "I'm twelve months sober and just as long celibate. Before that, I was a drunk on and off for the last seventeen years, pissing everyone off and leaving a trail of destruction behind me. I grew up in a strict Christian household with a ruthless, exacting preacher for a father and a complaisant mother, neither of whom have approved of me for the last twenty years or spoken to me in five, because I broke their hearts with my addiction. I'm here rediscovering myself as part of my recovery. I'm keeping the world safe from the curse that is Beckette Sl— me."

Jude fell even further toward his inevitable

love trap, if that were possible in three days. "Is it working?"

He glanced at her and paused. A small smile caught the corner of his mouth. "At times." He toyed with the sleeve of her robe. "I'm a bad bet, Jude Duffy. I'm an addict. An adrenaline junkie who thrives on chaos then self-destructs, taking down everyone around me while I drink to relieve the stress. I need to avoid messy attachments and keep to a steady, straight road so my stress level can be non-existent."

"There is no such thing as a stress-free world, Beck. You need to find inner peace against the outside stressors. Hence the word *inner*."

"Easier said than done."

"You didn't mention your wife." She studied the remoteness in his amber eyes. She should run like hell, but her inquisitive mind wanted to know the whole story about her beast.

"My wife?"

"Yes."

He paused, eyes lowered to his scarred hand. "I killed her six years ago."

Jude chuckled. "Stop. Tell me the truth. Maybe it will make you feel better to get it out."

He brought his gaze back to hers, the shadows misting through his eyes like dark clouds before a thunderstorm.

"You're telling me what you believe. Now tell me what happened."

He crossed his arms and backed to the opposite counter a few feet away, putting virtual miles between them. "She died a year after we were married because I was a drunken asshole who'd deserted her when she needed me to stay and work things out."

There was more to the story. She'd bet her life on it. She reached out, pulled him closer then touched the scar on his cheek. "You loved her."

He shrugged. "And I killed her. I keep a gun and a bottle of whiskey by my bed. Reminders of how quickly I could change my life if I chose."

Every part of her wanted to touch him, hold this shattered man, find out the whole story. "Let's hold off on those kind of changes for a while, hmmm?"

Beck smiled. "*You've* changed things. Some."

"For the better, I hope?"

He laughed. A wonderful, rusty chuckle. "The jury's still out." His features sobered. "You're dangerous to me, Jude."

"And the scars on your face and arm? How did you get those?"

He stood there, never taking his eyes from her, reading her, deciding…something. "All just reminders of the people I've hurt."

Jude ran her finger along his hand—puckered, filled with peaks and valleys to trap the pain. "My parents died in a plane crash. I know what it's like to feel guilt and sorrow over things said or unsaid before those we care about leave us. Some bad things just happen, Beck. Through no cause of our own."

He lifted his hands to her face, his eyes riveted to her lips. "Very dangerous."

His features hardened—in anger, fear, regret…she didn't know. But the intensity of his need enveloped her like the warmth of a steam shower as he lowered his lips to hers.

And she was done.

Done with worrying, done with researching, done with calculating, done with thinking. All she wanted was to feel.

His kiss was soft, yet demanding. His

tongue warm and commanding as he tasted her lips. She opened for him and his tongue swept inside like a marauder conquering his most arduous rival.

He pulled back abruptly and rested his forehead against hers. "Jude, the things I want to do to you. God, do you know how bad I am for you?"

She knew.

"I can't resist you. All I can think about is being with you, knowing you, fucking you."

She gasped and he smiled.

"Does that scare you?"

She shook her head. "Actually, no. Your dirty talk is...*stimulating*. I've never been with a man, Beck. My whole life has been on the outside looking in. I want to be inside that world. If only for a night, I'll take it."

His eyes narrowed. "But you don't want me. You want Fantome."

"I was hoping for a more clandestine affair. One where I didn't...*know* so much about my despoiler. An affair strictly of the body."

He rubbed his thumb over her bottom lip. "So honest, so innocent, so articulate." He tilted his head. "I wonder if you'll be chatty while I fuck you. I think I'd like that. To hear all your thoughts, everything you feel while I taste you, pump inside you over and over. Make you come."

He smiled then took her mouth in a ravenous kiss as he yanked her hips forward. Her robe fell open, exposing her satin night gown. The firm ridge of his erection pressed against her pelvis as if she had nothing on at all. It was marvelous.

Beck's hands moved up the sides of her waist to the underside of her breasts. The calluses on his large strong hands caught on the satin material as he held her, his thumbs stroking her aching nipples. Gosh darn. With the way his foreplay made her shiver and ache and tingle in her secret places, she hoped it lasted a lot longer than three minutes. Practice did make perfect and, as a researching scientist, she settled for nothing less than perfect.

Her beast lowered his head and suckled one of her breasts right through her nightgown. So glorious, so warm and wet. He groaned as he took her nipple between his teeth and bit down. That groan sent a bolt of lightning to her vaginal tissues, causing them to throb and moisten…biology at its best.

"Oh my God, Beck. That is wonderful." She

wriggled on the cold steel, pushing closer to his erection. He obliged, wrapping his arms around her hips and forcefully drawing her against him. Possessive and demanding, he rubbed his hard shaft against her clitoris. The response was instant. A throb, an electrical current lit up her girl parts, making her yearn to be touched. Holy God, her body *did* work. But what about the orgasm? When was the orgasm going to happen? This was lovely, but how was she to get there?

Jude started to fret. "Beck, I need, I need…"

He tilted her chin to catch her gaze. "Baby, I know just what you need." He slid her robe off her shoulders, taking the straps of her nightgown with it.

She caught the front and held it to her chest, embarrassed by her fleshy curves. Men in the twenty-first century did not prefer fleshy women. "I'm not a thin girl."

He smiled. "That's good, cause I don't like thin girls. They stopped appealing to me when I was twelve."

She laughed.

"You are just the type of girl I want. Soft and delicious." He swept her messy curls from her face. "With a beautiful mind." His brows arched. "And very clean hands."

She sighed and closed her eyes. "For how long, Beckette? How long could a mating like this possibly last?" Why ask such a question? She didn't really want the tragic response.

"I'm hoping it will last until I can make you come so many times you won't be able to walk."

Jude gasped. Did he just say that? Was that even possible?

Beck pulled her hands from her chest, causing her nightgown to fall from her large breasts. She tensed, waiting for his rejection.

"My God, you're gorgeous." The reverence in his voice sent hope skyrocketing through her soul. He lifted the skirt of the gown and abruptly tore her panties. They came off with a pinch to her hip, and he tucked them into his jeans' pocket. He kissed her then like he had something to prove, something to conquer. His tongue plundered every part of her mouth while his hands delicately stroked her breasts and taut nipples.

He bent, licking one aching nipple then the other, then pulled back and looked into her eyes. "I want to watch you come, Jude. I want to see those expressive eyes and that beautiful face and all it has to offer while you come. Will you come for me, honey?"

She stared, transfixed by his voice, his words, his politeness polished with a sinful decadence. "Yes." She nodded like an air-headed doll. Her lateral orbitofrontal cortex had just checked out.

He smiled and slid his hand up her bare thighs toward the throbbing mess of her womanhood. Jude didn't like messes. She instinctively closed her legs.

"No chance, Baby." The beast stepped closer, opening her knees wide with his hips, spreading her thighs with both hands. "You are beautiful, Jude. Warm, wet, needy. I always want you like this when you are around me. Will you do that for me? Always need me?"

It was more than a sexual request. Jude knew it as well as she knew she didn't have much of a choice. Every time she was near this man, smelled this man, thought of this man, she was going to weep with wanting him. He'd cast his sensual curse all over her.

"Yes." She pulled his mouth to hers. The kiss was demanding and urgent. A carnal merging of two lost souls.

Beck ended the kiss on a groan and slowly slid his fingers between her legs— a mating of flesh and fluids meant for the gods. His wicked fingers played and stroked her folds until he found her clitoris. He expertly rolled the little bundle of nerves into a throbbing, aching time bomb that needed to detonate.

Jude moaned, eyes closed as she focused on the glorious sensations.

"Open your eyes, Baby. I need to see everything going on in that brilliant mind." His voice wrapped around her like a warm velvet cocoon, scattering every one of her inhibitions and preconceived notions of what to expect. For once in her life, she just…Let. It. Be.

Jude blinked. Was there love in his gaze? Couldn't be in just three short days, but she swore…

Those talented nimble fingers slipped inside her. She was slick and swollen and craving his touch.

He owned her, held her prisoner between his hands—one pushing her lower back, the other palming her from the front. "Jude, I'm going to fuck you. I need to have you even though I know I shouldn't."

The nerve endings between her legs throbbed with joy. A responsive spasm answered his declaration. Was this it? The beginning of the mysterious 'O?' How marvelous! The vulgarity of his words should have turned her off, but his desperation seemed nothing short of reverence. Reverence for her.

He moaned, then quickly pulled his fingers from her depths and dropped his forehead to hers. "You will not come until you are around my dick. We are going to make love until we both forget who and what we are."

Holy crap, this strong, sexually-aroused alpha male was taking control as she sat there, spread open and half naked like a strumpet high on Viagra. "Yes. Yes, please. Hurry, Beck."

He smiled, then licked the finger he'd used inside her like an orgasmic weapon. He rubbed that finger over her bottom lip and, as her tongue touched her lip, she tasted herself. *Oh. My. God.*

Beck stepped back, lifted her off the table and cradled her to his chest.

"Beckette!"

"I may be a beast, but I'm not making love to you in a public kitchen. What I'm going to do to you isn't fit for onlookers."

"But the counter! I have to clean the counter! It's dirty, unsanitary with what we just did!"

"Baby, you haven't seen dirty yet."

Twelve

"I have just got a new theory of eternity."
Albert Einstein

Beck plopped her on his bed then stood back and stared.

Jude was nervous, exposed, lacking.

He smiled—a smile so sinister and calculating and filled with potential for debauchery, she tingled all over again between her legs.

He wanted her. He wanted Jude Duffy. Boring, inexperienced Jude Duffy.

Her eyes were drawn to his long fingers. Fingers that had just been inside her as he unbuttoned his jeans and pulled them down around his hips. His penis protruded, strong, hard, and ready. She'd never seen anything like it. Not even in the porn magazines she'd just

115

purchased. It was so beautiful she needed to touch it, reached with both hands and took hold of the warm, satiny, rock-hard appendage.

His head dropped back and he moaned. Jude liked that. She, Jude Duffy, had made this sexual beast moan. It was empowering.

She lifted her eyes to his sensual gaze. "What do I do? Teach me."

Beck's jaw clenched as he inhaled deeply. He placed his hand over hers and guided her to stroke him, where to touch him, how to make love to him.

She wanted more.

Joy rippled through her veins. She studied the magnificent penis in her hands as a small bead of semen leaked from the soft shiny head. She had the most unsanitary, compulsive, deviant need to taste. The desire to run her tongue over the velvety head. To explore the hard shaft with her lips.

So she did.

And it was absolute.

Absolute beauty, absolute trust, absolute passion, an absolute yearning to bring love and solace to this injured man.

She tasted and suckled, exploring every inch

of his hunger for her. This wasn't a physical act. It was emotional, passionate...covetous.

"Enough!" He pulled her to her feet and kissed her with abandon, his cock rubbing against her wet swollen tissues. "I need to be inside you. I've got to feel you wrapped around me, holding me, grounding me."

Jude closed her eyes. No nervousness, no dread, just sheer awe.

"Don't close your eyes. We're in this together. Are you sure this is what you want?" His amber eyes were laced with lust and restraint as he waited for her consent.

She nodded and looked down between them as he slipped on a condom. A small thread of disappointment ran through her. Protection. But it was okay. She didn't want to drag this wonderful man into her hair-brained scheme.

He wrapped his hand around his massive erection and pressed her back onto the bed. He settled his warm, hard body over hers, his weight a magnificent pressure. He stilled until she looked into his eyes.

"You are so beautiful." He rubbed the head of his penis through her juices in a circular motion, stroking her clit, inciting her once again to a throbbing bundle of sensation. He grimaced in pleasure as he pushed the head of his penis inside her.

She inhaled sharply, her head tilted back. It was beautiful, soft, hard, filling…heavenly.

She never knew.

He stroked in and out of her a mere inch, gently probing and massaging her, driving her to the brink of madness, his whiskey gaze frozen on hers.

Jude clasped his cheeks. "Beck. It feels so good. Please." She wrapped her feet around his hips and tried to draw him deeper.

"I don't want to hurt you, Baby. We have to go slow. I want this to be good for you."

She smiled. "It's already too good."

He groaned and plunged deep, tearing through her hymen with little pain, much to her surprise. He held her close, not moving, breathing deep, and filling her. "Are you okay, Baby?"

Baby. She liked that. She'd never had a nickname.

"I will be, once you give me my first orgasm." His smile shifted her hair, and she braced for his rebuttal.

It didn't come with words. It came with an anchoring of her body by his hands and the most beautiful, athletic cadence of a pair of men's hips she'd ever imagined. He slid into her, stroking her, commanding her, making love to her. He rammed through her tissues like a wild man—one second possessed, the next sensually exploring every inch of her with his erotic, rhythmic thrusts. She couldn't decide where to look, at his amber eyes so filled with wonder or the intimidating weapon, covered with her juices as it plunged in and out of her. Both were so beautiful.

A tingling, a tightening in her lower abdomen built toward her clit. She pulled him closer, burying her face in his neck, squeezing her stomach muscles, hoping to push all the energy in her body toward that one glorious spot. She inhaled his spicy, musky scent as she reached for the pinnacle. Did one just wait? Did she have to do something to hit the crescendo? She didn't know what to do. Was it this way for other women?

"Baby, I'm going to come so hard inside you. God, you feel amazing." Beck shoved to his elbows, looking into her eyes as he grasped her face in his hands. "Do you feel me? Do you feel what you do to me? After this, I'm going to taste you. Every part of you. I'm going to lick you until you come in my mouth. But first, I need to feel you come around my cock. I need it so badly, Jude."

His forehead dropped to hers and his eyes closed as he ground his hips into hers.

Jude clenched her arms around him, her heart bursting with love that flowed through her body, settling in the place where they joined. The heat began like a lightning storm in her limbs, every joint, then shot directly to her core as it ripped through her body. The shock of a blinding orgasm enveloped her. "Beck. Oh God, oh God, I'm orgasming. Am I orgasming? Is this it? Oh God, it feels so good, please don't stop!"

The man laughed as he drew out her pleasure with the same sexy rhythm. "That's it, Baby. Take me. All of me. Let me feel you."

He wanted to feel her!

"Jude, that is so good, so beautiful, honey."

The rush of a million shooting stars shot through her veins, from the top of her head to her pulsing vaginal tissues. It was glorious as she spasmed around him, over and over, the intense throbbing like nothing she'd ever experienced before, and wanted to again and again.

The crescendo quieted. The pulsing slowed, spacing.

It was…*amazing*.

His hands surrounded her face. She opened her eyes and looked into the most beautiful amber storm.

"You liked that," he stated. So confident.

"I did."

He let out a quiet, satisfied chuckle. "Baby, you are so beautiful all sated and happy, but I need to come inside you. I can't wait any longer."

He lifted his body for leverage, the muscles in his chest and shoulders contracting like a magnificent beast as he groaned and pumped furiously into her. The strong, throbbing pulsations of his penis mesmerized her. He was marking her, changing her. His face contorted in ecstasy just before he threw his head back and ejaculated over and over inside her, pumping his seed into the condom that kept him safe from her nefarious ideas.

"Jude, oh God, Baby." He collapsed on top of her, the warmth of his skin, the beating of his heart, comforting her. She wrapped her arms around him and held him close, shoving her love down, down, down. Back to the depths of her subconscious where she didn't have to face it.

If she did, she'd have to concede that love at first sight existed, which it didn't. It had only been three days. Besides, her heart would break when he left her, and she'd had enough heartbreak for a lifetime.

She allowed herself one small moment to relish the acceptance, this connection, then pushed at his muscular shoulders to get him off of her.

He lifted his head and frowned. "What? Am I hurting you?"

"No, I have to go. I forgot to disinfect the ice bucket in my room."

He smirked then lowered his lips to hers and kissed her into submission. The man was a master. Way out of Jude's league. She gave in like a starving woman. A woman in love.

But he'd never love her. Love was one of those frivolous emotions, fleeting with most human beings. She'd get over him like she had all the rest who'd left her. She had to.

Now that she'd nurtured visions of holidays

and school conferences and summer vacations with a child, *her* child, she couldn't go back. She had to continue on her quest with a vengeance. Time was running out.

She pushed him away. "Thank you so much, Beckette. I truly enjoyed myself." *And have fallen hopelessly in love with you.* She twisted and tried to wiggle out from under his large naked body, making her escape before those words found their way to her lips.

"Enjoyed?"

She stilled at the sarcasm in his voice. "Why yes, it was quite enjoyable. The orgasm was even more than I expected. You know, almost seventy-five percent of woman never reach orgasm from intercourse alone. Most need the help of tools, hands, or tongue. Your job here is done."

A growl emanated from the depths of his chest. He captured her lips again and pulled her underneath him. He truly was a beast. Her beast, if only for tonight. He pulled back and smiled, and she swore his incisors had lengthened. "Honey, we've only just begun."

* * * *

Beckette had never experienced anything as

erotic as sex with Jude.

The woman talked the whole way through, all three times he'd reached for her during the night. She told him what she wanted, everything she felt, what she wanted to learn from him. She was innocent, refreshing, and truly sensual. He'd never been with anyone like her and, most likely, would never be with her again.

After tonight, he'd let her go research her newfound excitement with another man. Another man who would taste her, feel her innocence and love.

He groaned, pulling her back to his chest. The warmth of her velvet skin…her tangy essence when she'd come in his mouth. She let out a sleepy groan and snuggled her ass against him.

He lifted her leg, opening her to enter from behind. She was still wet, still so warm and welcoming. She was heaven wrapped tightly around him, as he slowly pumped into her. He didn't know how he'd ever let her go, but he would. He didn't do love, and this woman was all about love. She deserved it and he couldn't give it to her.

So, instead, he took this moment to revel in her brilliance, her acceptance. Something he didn't deserve.

Her lush body was a wonderland of sensation. So responsive as she writhed against him in time with his pleading strokes.

"Beck…" she whispered and convulsed around him. This woman was made for sex.

He nuzzled her hair, allowing his dick to enjoy every contraction of her pulsing wet channel. "Baby, I'm going to come so hard inside you. Do you want me to come inside you? Are you protected?"

She reached over her head and grabbed his hair. "Yes, please. Beck, please!"

He thanked the Lord for birth control then slammed his hips into her, giving her everything he was, as he erupted deep inside her.

Suddenly, she pulled away. "Wait. Oh no, wait!" She rolled onto her back and he grabbed himself and stroked, finishing on her stomach. Her eyes widened as his dick pulsed, spurting his semen across her skin.

"Jesus H. Christ, woman!" He finished and flopped on top of her, exhausted from one of the most powerful orgasms he'd ever had.

Jude leaped off the bed and paced, his come glistening on her beautiful skin. He was an animal for enjoying the view of his mark on her.

"I…I had no idea it was so late. I need to go."

He didn't want her to go. He wanted the heaven he'd experienced inside her again, the bliss of being buried inside her with no barrier numbing his dick.

Yeah, he was a fiend. A beast.

"I don't want you to go." Was all he could think of to say.

She paced toward the bathroom and returned with a washcloth, glaring at him over the vigorous scrubbing she gave her gorgeous body.

"I kind of liked the sight of my come on your stomach. Now you've ruined all my fantasies for the day."

She snorted. "You're a Neanderthal." She bent and began to dress. Much to his dismay. This isn't how he wanted their short affair to end.

* * * *

Jude pulled on her nightgown and robe, avoiding eye contact with Beckette. Her mind spun as her feet carried her back to the bed of sin, and she furiously tugged at the sheets where she'd lost her virginity…and her heart. She'd thought by *protected*, he'd meant her heart. How could she have been so stupid?

She stripped the sheets right out from under him. "Thank you so much for all you've done." She'd almost let this man ejaculate inside her. Forging a child together would decimate his trust in her…and her self-respect.

He rose and stood silently on the opposite side of the bed, his powerful arms crossed as if he were proud of his nakedness. He'd be devastated by her lack of appreciation right now. She was supposed to be lying in his arms like a warm, satiated kitten or something. At least that's what she'd read in her books, but panic wouldn't allow her to bask in the glow.

Jude glanced up at him as she bundled the sheets into a ball.

He cocked a beastly brow. "What do you think you're doing?"

"Cleaning up. Then leaving. You quite exhausted me." All she could think about was getting to her room to use vaginal cleanser and hopefully eradicate any and all of his sperm before they fertilized her egg. She would not do this to him. She wouldn't do this to herself. Not now that she'd…fallen for him?

Her heart clenched. She lifted the bundle and marched toward the door. "I'll have these cleaned for you."

"Wait!"

She turned back to him and he held out her torn jacket. "I fixed the pocket."

Jude's heart fractured, her stomach sank and all her dreams of having a baby flew right out the window. How could she be so unethical and disloyal and careless as to mistakenly trap a man she cared about? And how could she even consider sharing something so intimate and poignant with someone else?

She couldn't.

Her heart was lost forever to this man. This sweet, damaged man who'd shown her what love was really about. It wasn't about dinners and fancy flowers and expensive rings. Love wasn't a thing. It was when the one she loved sat in his cold, lonely room in the basement and sewed a patch on her favorite coat.

Thirteen

"I never think of the future—
it comes soon enough."
Albert Einstein

A loud banging rattled the door to her suite, and Jude's breakfast rose in her throat.

"Jude Duffy, open this goddamned door right now!" *Beckette.* Each vicious knock thumped through her heart. "Did you think I wouldn't find out?"

Find out what?

She rose from the bed and opened the door to be faced with a raging lunatic.

"You were trying to trap me by getting pregnant with my child?"

His words stopped the aching, fluttering organ in her chest. "I-I'm sorry, but that's not actually how it is." All the guilt and shame rose through her body like lava rising through the ashes of a volcano. She was despicable.

He stormed into the room and threw a beautiful bouquet of sweet peas and lavender on the floor. "That's not what the sex shop girl had to say. She works at the florist, too. She said you had big plans to have sex so you could get pregnant!" He spun to face her. "Could you be pregnant? Was I just part of your ridiculous plan?"

She brought her eyes to his, stormy and dark, filled with loathing. She didn't want this wonderful man to loathe her. What had she done?

She turned her back to him and paced. She needed to reason this all out. "Maybe, yes…no… Oh, I don't know! I douched and cleansed and did everything I could when I got back to my room to prevent pregnancy."

His mouth dropped open. "The idea of having my kid was so disgusting that you douched? What, did you want Fantome's kid more?"

She'd hurt him. "No. No, I just…just." Anger rose like a burning flame. After all the time they'd spent getting to know each other, he thought she was this wretched?

She sat on the bed and took a deep breath. She had been wretched. Shamefully idiotic with her whole plan. She'd come to her senses, given up on all of it since they'd been together. He'd showed her she was worthy of love. Someone was out there for her. She wanted the whole package.

Her eyes met his as he stood over her, his big arms crossed.

Honesty. That was what she was good at. "Yes, I wanted a baby, but not with you."

He flinched, but she didn't back down. He deserved the truth.

"I originally had this horrible realization I would be alone for the rest of my life." She pleaded into his eyes for understanding.

"So you figured you'd get pregnant and trap me into some fairy tale of yours? Been there, done that."

She shook her head. "No. I didn't want to have sex with you. Ever. At least, not after I got to know you. I tried to stay away from you, Beckette. I didn't want to hurt you."

"Why? I'm not good enough? Rich enough? A blue collar, recovering alcoholic isn't acceptable to a big scientist like you?"

"Because I'd fallen in love with you!" She cut off his tirade.

A windstorm picked up in his beautiful golden eyes. His nostrils flared and his jaw clenched. "Don't love me, Jude Duffy. You have no idea who I am, how I'm capable of destroying you."

He turned and slammed the door shut on yet another frivolous dream in Jude's life.

Fourteen

"Insanity: doing the same thing over and over again and expecting different results."
Albert Einstein

"You look beautiful."

Jude ran her hands over the vintage gown Nola had loaned her—a celadon green silk, tight in the beaded bodice with an open squared neck that barely held Jude's bust.

"Beck feels a great responsibility for his wife's death, you know. She lied to him about a pregnancy. He married her and then, six months later, he realized the truth." Nola handed Jude the matching mask.

Jude stroked the beads sewn along the edge, her chest aching. She had almost done the same thing to him. How deep his anger must truly be. "I didn't know."

"He doesn't talk about it. They fought. He got drunk, lost his temper and refused to remain home to work things out. He left to join his friends at some bar where the band he played with sometimes performed. When he returned home the next morning, she'd killed herself."

Tears filled Jude's eyes. Tears for the compassionate, damaged man she'd fallen in love with.

"He hasn't sung in front of anyone since then. Except you. You're good for him. He might even forgive himself if he can get out of his own way and admit your love could be the key to his salvation."

"He has to save himself. I don't know if I'll even see him tonight. He doesn't attend the guest events." She didn't know if she even wanted to see him. He obviously didn't have the same feelings for her but, perhaps, she needed to be sure before she gave up on love…again.

She refused to be a coward any longer. Beck had taught her that.

Nola smiled. "Then you'll just have to find him."

With a nod, Jude took a deep breath and crossed to the door to make her way to the

Monster Ball.

He had to listen. He had to understand. She wouldn't take no for an answer.

It was her time. Her chance to go after something she wanted.

And, more than anything, she wanted to be brave and frivolous enough to pursue her dreams, make her beast see how truly special he was.

* * * *

Beckette put the finishing touches on his costume while Ennis sat on the bed and *supervised*. Beck was finally back to his old life, in front of the camera, acting, pretending, forgetting.

If only he could forget about her.

She'd used him. Just like Elizabeth. He wouldn't go through that again.

But it hurt like hell. Hopefully, seeing him in his element tonight would put an end to her foolish fantasies. His real name would be announced to all the guests who had come to know him as Handy Man Beck.

She'd remember Gabriel Beckette Slauter, the pilot who'd taken her parents from her. And she'd despise him, leave him, and keep herself safe from the curse that was Beckette Slader. Then he'd be able to return to his lonely life, fighting his daily demons, repenting through Angel Wings and a busy, non-fulfilling acting career that let him pretend he was someone else fifteen hours a day.

None of that changed what he'd done, however. Accidents? No, he'd caused the deaths of three people and would spend the rest of his days suffering the guilt.

"You're being an ass, you know. You're stronger than you think." This, from a twenty-year-old gardener. Ennis expertly tied the silk ascot around Beck's neck.

Beck glanced down at the fitted charcoal jacket and black knickers the kid had pulled from his quirky wardrobe. "I can't believe you had Hessian boots that fit me. And what would you know about relationships, Ennis? You're barely out of diapers."

His protégé smirked and placed his hands on his hips. Ennis dressed weird but, considering he was straight off the boat from Ireland, Beck figured maybe it was a European thing to love vintage crap. Just looked like old crap to him.

"Do you love her?"

Beck swallowed—his spit, his words and his feelings. He was good at that. "It doesn't matter."

"Be gad! It's the only thing that matters." Ennis' Irish brogue was thicker tonight than usual. Jack Daniels? "Yer always acting the plike, fella."

"Love doesn't cure all things, Ennis."

"The right love can, bloke. And if you don't figure that out soon, you'll be a lonely eegit." Ennis turned. "Love is a verb, Beckette. You'd be surprised the things it can help you do and overcome. When we find that someone who makes us feel our best, we can conquer anything."

"She'll realize she doesn't love me when she finds out who and what I really am."

"It's you, who has to figure out who and what you really are. You've been living under false pretenses." Ennis slipped out the door just as it opened.

"What are you mumbling about?" Ava Callahan walked into Beck's room and wrapped her arms around him from behind. She rested her chin on his shoulder and stared at herself in the mirror. Such a shallow girl, but she was a good agent. "That simpering redhead? Beckette, it's time you got your head on straight and got over her. She's no one to you."

He handed her a mask that matched the one Alana had given him. "Let's get this done."

She smiled. "Tonight's a special night. I've got a big surprise for you. Tonight and forever on, is ours."

* * * *

For the first time in her life, Jude was stunned into complete silence. And not in a good way.

She stood in the doorway of the beautifully decorated ballroom in her vintage finest, seething at the traitorous thoughts of life, love and family that had floated through her mind the past few days.

She had only wanted to belong, be part of something wonderful. To have someone to love and have them love her in return.

Frivolous, futile thoughts.

It was all over now—the wishing, the hoping, the fairy tale. She'd faced the cold hard truth standing on that podium, being interviewed by Harry Strubel, the TV marauder who had ruined her life with the help of her ex-fiancé.

Beckette, whatever the hell his name was,

had used her. Used her like a dirty stool he could step on to reach the pinnacle of fame.

He must have known all along about her downfall on the *Harry Strubel Show*. He'd never let on, the clever sadist, but his plan had worked. Her notoriety with the famous celebrity interviewer was now adding to Beck's fame. Just like it had with Evan.

Jude stared at the charismatic turncoat as he stood onstage in the middle of the ornately decorated room. Beckette was the center of attention, all poise and charm. The quiet loner of her heart was gone. Harry Strubel interviewed this stranger about his new role in an upcoming movie…and his humorous tryst with the pitiful "Honey, you're nice, but I like his package better than yours" girl.

She didn't hear his words. All eyes were upon her, the smirks, the pity, the sorrow, the laughter. She'd always been the butt of jokes. Her eccentric childhood, her strange mind, her complete failure as a scientist and woman.

She shifted her gaze to the life-size glossy posters. Beck in his former acting roles and with former leading ladies, parties, and fame. He wasn't the sweet, quiet, maintenance man she'd fallen in love with. The man who played the piano in the dark. The man who built beautiful things with his hands. The man who'd mended her jacket and her heart.

Jude processed the name—his real name— written in big letters. Beckette Slader. She knew that name.

Beckette Slader was none other than Gabriel Beckette Slauter. The boy who'd crashed her parents' plane.

She took a deep breath, and met his hypnotic gaze for a fraction of a second. He made no move toward her. No hint of remorse ghosted in his stoic, hardened features. This was a man who didn't care.

She turned and fled.

* * * *

Beck's anger grew to thundering heights as he took in the satisfied smirks of Fantome and his bitch-of-an-agent, Ava Callahan. They'd done this. They'd set him up. He'd had no idea Jude's broken engagement had been a national topic on the *Harry Strubel Show*. He hadn't watched TV since he'd been here.

But, knowing Jude, the negative attention it had brought to her and her work had devastated her. No wonder she'd been acting so out of character all week. She had PTSD, for Christ's sake. And now he'd added to it. *Monster.*

His gaze traveled the room as he frantically looked for Jude. He caught one quick glimpse of her agonized features and the tear that slid from her beautiful eyes just before she turned and ran, her dress billowing behind her.

Beck's first instinct was to jump off the stage and chase after her. But he didn't. He held his place, *this* place in front of thousands of fans. Where he could be a stranger to them and himself. Where he didn't have to face his injustices and guilt. Here, he could be someone else. This was where he belonged.

It was better this way.

He needed this and she didn't.

She needed someone different. Someone who didn't wreck lives and drink himself into ten-day benders when things got tough. She needed someone who could trust and love. Who could love her wholly, with all they had.

All he had to give her were reservations. He wasn't whole.

He was a beast. A Dr. Jekyll who could turn into Mr. Hyde.

The chatter continued as he signed

autographs and shook hands for what seemed like hours, successfully restraining the vehement temptation to run to her.

"Do you love her?"

Shut up, Ennis.

"It's the only thing that matters."

I said shut up, Ennis!

"You'd be surprised the things love can do and help you overcome…"

Beck left the stage and made his exit, toward her, away from Ennis, away from Strubel and Ava… He didn't know.

"Where the hell do you think you're going?" Ava whispered tightly over his shoulder. "This is a publicity event for *you*!"

"I need to get out of here." He fucking hated the publicity part of this career.

"It's her, isn't it? You're going after her."

He turned toward the hurt and rage in his agent's voice. Richard Fantome stood behind her, smirking.

"You knew about her association with Strubel didn't you?"

Ava's mouth opened, but nothing came out.

"I'm outta here." He spun to leave.

Alcohol beckoned him like a siren's call. It would numb the pain, silence the taunts. Release the stress about to blow his head off. All because of *emotional ties.*

"This is your career, Beck. You wanted this. *We* wanted this. I've worked too hard and been with you too long. She can't have you."

"Well, neither can you."

Fifteen

*"It is strange to be known so universally
and yet to be so lonely."*
Albert Einstein

He pitied her.

He'd tolerated her and slept with her out of pity for killing her parents. A consolation prize for her troubles.

Jude ambled along the top floor hallway, ancient portraits of people important to the castle's history, staring at her from every angle. She'd never been here before, but had been told the maids' quarters were on this floor.

She needed to return Nola's dress and get back to her small apartment in New York. To figure out what she should do with the rest of her life.

Loneliness weighed heavy on her heart. It

had been nothing but her work for so long. No real friends, no family…

Loving someone and being betrayed forged a desolation like no other. Yes, Evan had betrayed her, but she'd never really loved him. She'd never been loved by him, either. That was the difference. Losing the soul-deep comfort of being fully accepted for who she was by Beckette, was like having every vein pulled from her body, one by one. A loss so great, she was afraid she'd bleed to death without anyone even noticing.

She ran her hand over the old canvases, the rigid strokes rough under her fingertips. Such history, so many mysteries and lives come and gone.

Would she ever leave a mark on this world in any way? Would anyone remember her and carry on her heart?

A cold draft blew across Jude's shoulders, and she shivered. It didn't matter that Beckette had been the pilot when her parents' plane had gone down. He'd been a kid. Made a tremendous mistake.

That was in the past.

Hiding his identity from her… It was

laughable. Using her to assuage his guilt, hiding behind his acting career to run from his past and his addiction. That was sad. She knew what it was like to use work as a way to avoid the difficulties of life and relationships. She was guilty of that herself.

But then Beck had taken things to a whole new level. He'd included her failures in his debauchery, had enchanted her, then drained her joy like a vampire, just to save his career.

She could never go back. Love at first sight? Ridiculous.

Another cold breeze gusted through the dark hallway. Jude glanced around for an open window, but found none. The smell of lavender floated in the air as she peered down the hall toward an open door and lighted room.

"Jude!"

She jumped. She didn't want to see him, didn't want to talk or hear his explanations and apologies. She was tired and just wanted to catch the next train home to safety.

She turned to face him, his appearance as beautiful and haunted as ever.

"Did you have to pity me?" She crossed her arms and breathed deep to hold back her tears.

She had so many emotions, so many issues with this whole mess, she didn't know where to start. But she wasn't a coward when it came to speaking her mind. "Did you really think having sex with me would make me feel better? Did you do it so you could get on the *Harry Strubel Show* and further your career?"

His brows lowered in a confused frown. "What do you mean?"

"The sex, the charming man, the friend who took me out of all my comfort zones and showed me how to be...*me*. How to not be afraid of trying new things. Did you do all that because you thought you owed me something for killing my parents?" She sighed. "My parent's deaths were a long time ago, Beck. An accident. You were an immature kid. It was nothing you did purposefully. Not like what you did tonight."

He ran a hand through his disheveled hair. "You're upset."

"You're damned right, I'm upset. You're a coward. A slithering coward."

"Me?"

She huffed. "At least I'm not afraid to take a shot at love. To be open and honest about my flaws. Tragedy happens, Beck. That doesn't

147

mean people should stop living. Quit playing the victim."

His eyes opened wide, and he scoffed. "I'm just being smart, here. Somebody has to be logical."

"I'll take love and passion over logic any day. You taught me that. Do you love me at all, Beck?"

He stared. His features hardened.

"That's what I thought." She turned her back on him.

"Wait. It's only been a week. Six days ago, I couldn't even decide between ravioli or linguini." Jude turned to face him and he sighed. "Do you actually believe you could fall in love with me in such a short time?"

"I do. Unlike you, I'm a hopeless romantic on an optimistic streak this week. Next week, I might very well hate you, so we're good to go."

A storm brewed in his golden eyes. "You want honesty? This," he touched his cheek, "is from Elizabeth. She hit me with one of my broken beer bottles during a fight we had because I was a drunken bastard who didn't give a shit. And the burns," he rubbed his arm, "are from the plane crash where I killed your parents.

I drank that day, and they are all reminders of my destructiveness."

Jude's lungs constricted, and she sucked in much-needed air. "I don't know what your parents did to you to make you think you don't deserve forgiveness, but you are not in control of all the bad things that happen in the world. You made mistakes in the past, but you're a better man now. Live up to it."

His lips thinned, and he tipped his head back to stare at the ceiling.

Jude sighed. "You know what? It's really okay. I understand. I'm not one to run away sniveling and crying over some situation I fully participated in. You can go back to your fans and your life. I'm fine."

She marched quickly down the corridor, ignoring the blank stares of the dead patrons preserved on canvas. She made it to the lighted room where she hoped to find Nola.

"Jude, we're not finished!"

"Yes, we are!" She couldn't stand to be near him. It only broke her heart more. She couldn't stand to hear his excuses for why he didn't love her or why he couldn't love himself.

She stopped just inside a cavernous room

that must have been meant for private parties, turned to send Beck on his way, and then froze at the sight of Ava Callahan over Beckett's shoulder.

The woman teetered down the hall on her four inch heels. Her face twisted in fury, as the pistol she held toward the center of Beckette's back wavered through the air.

Jude screamed, understanding the woman's evil intent, then leaped in front of Beckette as the shot reverberated through the hall. Hot lava burned her chest and shoulders as she fell into Beckette, bringing him with her to the ground just inside the room. The metallic scent of blood filled her nostrils as she fought to breathe.

The warmth of the room enveloped her. Nola came, and a young man who held Nola tightly to his chest.

Was that Jude's celadon dress on Nola? It looked wonderful except for the blood stain across the bodice. Jude smiled. "Nola, you look beautiful. You have a bouquet of lavender. I love lavender."

"Who the hell is Nola? Oh God, Jude. Honey, what did you do?" Beckette's voice was harsh. He cradled her head and shoulders on his knees. "Honey, stay awake, you hear me? Stay with me."

His voice faded and Jude's pain diminished. She floated on a soft cloud, warmed by his body heat.

"Why, Jude? Why would you risk jumping in front of me?"

She looked at him, his features blurred slightly, and smiled. "You'd be surprised what a person is capable of, when they are in love."

He pulled her to his chest. Her gaze traversed the beautiful room until they landed on a strangely familiar portrait on the wall above the fireplace. That same spicy lavender wafted across her body as she tried to rise from Beck's lap for a closer look.

"Jude, honey, sit still until the ambulance gets here." He pressed harder against the wound in her chest. "I have to stop the bleeding."

Why was he crying? She didn't care about her sweater. All she cared about was the portrait. She lifted her head for a better look.

"It's Nola," she whispered.

"Who's Nola, Deary?" Alana…Alana Fitzgerald knelt next to her.

"My maid." The beautiful painting was Nola and the handsome man who'd held her in this room moments ago. Jude glanced around to find them, but they were gone. She pointed. "There, in the picture. That's Nola, my maid."

"No, honey, that is Nayeli. She was a Uti Indian princess, daughter of a chief back in the late 1800s."

Jude smiled at Alana. "And the man? Tell me about the man." She remembered his grief from her dream.

"Ennis McLoughlin was an Irish immigrant's son who fell in love with Nayeli. The chief planned to kill Nayeli for she was betrothed to an Indian warrior. Nayeli wanted to run away with Ennis, but convinced her father to end the betrothal to Akando. Folklore states that young Ennis met with her to end the relationship, to save her, not knowing she'd already saved herself. The warrior Akando followed Nayeli to the castle, overheard Ennis breaking Nayeli's heart and shot an arrow in an attempt to kill young Ennis for disgracing her."

"What happened?" Sirens wailed in the distance. Jude's thoughts faded and the room dimmed. The coldness was close to unbearable. "Tell me what happened, Alana."

"Nayeli jumped in front of Ennis, took the arrow for him and died in his arms, right here in this very room."

Jude cried, small and silent for the lovers, her maid. Her ghost maid. Such a silly concept. She was a scientist, but since falling mystically and hopelessly in love, anything seemed possible.

"What happened to Ennis?" The urgency in Beck's voice as he stroked Jude's hair intrigued her. She tried to focus on his pale features.

"Young Ennis killed himself that night. Hung himself in your room, Beckette. Nayeli had stayed in your room, Jude, the night before their tragic meeting in October, over two hundred years ago this very night. It is said all of these rooms are haunted by the lovers."

Jude reached up and touched Beck's cheek. "You know him, don't you?"

Beck smiled down at her. "Yes, I believe I do."

Jude closed her eyes as Beck held her and sang Hey Jude just for her.

Sixteen

"Once we accept our limits,
we go beyond them."
Albert Einstein

Jude packed her bags on the hospital bed, thrilled to be rid of it. After a week, she was sore, tired and ready to get home.

She hadn't seen Beck since he'd flown her to the university hospital in Aurora himself, in his own plane. The man was still full of secrets.

He'd dropped her off like a care package with nothing to remember him by but a bouquet of lavender, a get well card, and a now deflated *Beauty and the Beast* Mylar balloon.

Her heart ached. Who would have thought a week in a fairy tale castle could bring such excitement and tenderness. Such love and devastation.

The place really was haunted.

She hoped Beckette had found everything he was looking for. Hoped he'd found a way to forgive himself, a way to love himself.

"You're leaving?"

She screeched and spun, taking in the handsome familiar form of the first man she'd ever loved. "Beckette."

"We need to talk."

She dropped her eyes and zipped her suitcase. "No, we don't."

"We do. I need to explain."

"There's nothing to explain, Beck. I need things you're not willing to give. God forbid, you have faith in yourself and accept my love and use it to heal."

He sighed. "I *am* sorry."

Jude tilted her head. "For what, exactly? Dropping me here like a used condom and not coming back all week? Or for not being able to love me because you think you're a cursed soul?"

"I was here every fucking day. I just couldn't look at how you were injured, almost dead, because of me."

"Stop being so self-centered. I wasn't shot

because of you. I was shot because of a crazy woman."

He raked both hands through his hair. "Give me a break here, Jude. Just because you throw your heart around doesn't mean I have to."

The man was an idiot. "It's called love, Beck. It's not a disease. And this is the first time for me, actually."

"Well you picked the wrong guy for your first time. I'm cursed, don't you see that? Everyone who gets near me is in danger. You got shot because of me."

"You're whining. It's unbecoming."

"I brought you into this because I wanted you, had to have you." He paced across the room and glanced out the window. "Love just isn't in my DNA. Alcoholism is."

She needed him gone. His excuses for why he didn't love her ripped her apart, but she'd never allow him the satisfaction of seeing it. "Alcoholism is a devastating disease, but it can be controlled, Beck. You can still live a full life." She zipped then lifted her suitcase from the bed. "Good luck with everything."

He faced her again. "Christ, you're awful serene. You sure you love me? Because, from where I'm standing, you look like a woman getting ready to sort laundry. I...I can't be what you want, Jude."

"Are you saying I'm needy?" She couldn't help her shrill tone. He was pissing her off.

He ran a scarred hand over his face. "Everything about you is needy. Those cat eyes, that centerfold body, that...that brain of yours. You scream 'take me, love me, be with me.' It's taking everything I have not to come over there and grab on to you for dear life."

Jude waited, hoping he'd recognize his ridiculousness.

"All of it makes me need you, and I don't want to need you. I shouldn't need anyone."

"Needing someone isn't bad, Beck. It's vulnerable. And vulnerability can be a good thing where love is involved."

He shook his head. "If I become vulnerable, I'll inevitably drag you down with me when I spiral. I can't do that to you, Jude. I can't do love or relationships. Especially with y—"

"Yeah, I know. But I'm a big strong girl, Beck." God, he made her feel worthless. "I know about my parents and I know about Elizabeth. And I still somehow love you and know you are a wonderful man. Amazing, isn't it? How destructive our self image can be? You're letting yours ruin your life."

"I killed her."

"Elizabeth killed herself. You had a fight. Something people do and then they work it out. Rational people don't kill themselves. You had no chance to save her, Beck. That was all on her. And the plane? You were a stupid, irresponsible kid. I think you feel enough remorse for a thousand people."

He locked his hands behind his head and exhaled forcefully.

Jude sighed. "You're good to go. No need to keep repeating yourself. I didn't ask you to come here, so stop with the guilt. I understand many love affairs terminate because the love one person has is not reciprocated by the other, and I'm okay with that. Look at poor Evan. I forgot about him the first minute I saw you, and your talents are nothing compared to Evan's skills with lip liner. And have you seen my surgeon? I'll be lucky to get out of here without him proposing to me again. He makes you look like Yoda. No offense. It took me a while to figure it out, but the opinions of the Harry Strubel's of this world don't mean shit to me anymore. I'm

Jude Duffy and I can swim!"

His crestfallen features were a façade she was sure he'd mastered in acting school. "What if I don't want you to go?"

"You'll either get over it or you'll man up and decide your demons don't feed off of love. They feed off your fear, and those fears can't be conquered unless you face them. You taught me that. You'll never know if you can overcome until you try, Beck."

She pressed a kiss to the corner of his mouth and forced a smile. "Now, I've got things to do. My Tantric massage therapist is waiting for me in New York." She'd be damned if she'd let him see her pain. Damned if she let him pity her or see her cry. "I won't be another man's millstone. I'm better than that. Take care and, hey, good luck with that career you hate but think you need."

"I do this for both of us, Judc!"

She shook her head in disbelief. "Not for me, you don't." There was no 'us'. There never had been. He'd made sure of that.

"The money has been going into your trust since I started acting fifteen years ago."

She stilled, her mouth dropping like a

guppy. "Well, you can take every damn pity penny back."

* * * *

The movie schedule was gruesome, the weather bleak and his life…meaningless.

Beck had spent the last month immersed in work, but nothing helped. He couldn't stop thinking of Dr. Jude Duffy.

Why, he had no idea.

Which was a lie.

His job was to be his focus, his rehab, where all his concentration and efforts could be channeled to keep the demons at bay.

But he'd never wanted to drown himself in alcohol more than he had the past thirty days.

At least I'm not afraid to love.

He crushed the empty can of Mountain Dew his new agent had handed him on his way back to his trailer. Jude just didn't get how the world worked.

I tried and things didn't work out. That's more than I can say for you.

He had tried, hadn't he? Didn't she know she deserved better?

Vulnerability can be a good thing where love is involved.

He flung open his trailer door and stomped in. His ever present JD bottle sat on the counter, taunting him.

You'll either get over it or you'll man up and decide your demons don't feed off of love. They feed off your fear, and those fears can't be conquered unless you face them.

He grabbed the bottle and smashed it against the wall. He didn't ache for alcohol. He found no joy in work. He only ached for the sight of her face, her touch and the joy and peace he'd found in her arms.

She'd changed him. Changed his view of who and what he really was. Who he could become. A good man, loved by her.

She was his new addiction. A positive one.

Finally.

He only hoped it wasn't too late.

* * * *

Intellectuals solved problems, geniuses were supposed to prevent them. *Like hell.* Einstein had been wrong. Geniuses created problems with their rapid fire ideas and god-awful judgment.

Jude rounded the bend in Central Park, mumbling to herself, then gasped.

A huge stage stood in the center of Sheep Meadow. In the middle of metal work and speakers, a man sat at a baby grand piano. A beast dressed in black.

Beckette.

She would've known him anywhere.

"Jude Duffy, this is for you." She drank in his molten voice through the mic as his soulful gaze met hers.

He began to play and the audience went completely silent. She recognized the song. One of her *Beatles* favorites. A song of love and change.

Maybe I'm Amazed.

His voice pierced her soul, as she plopped to the grass in shock.

Once it was over, when her heart lay on the ground splayed open, he rose and exited the stage toward her.

"You were a bit flat in the third chorus." Jude stood, her heart in her throat at the sight of him. "You're no Paul McCartney, you know. Not Ringo, even."

His features softened. "I haven't been sleeping much."

Jude shrugged. She needed to keep up her

defenses. "Partying will do that to a person."

She didn't want him here. Didn't want his guilt, his pity, his fishing line thrown out just so he could haul it back in before she bit. She couldn't go through the pain of loving and missing him again.

She was healing. She'd made a new life for herself. Her career as a children's book author was taking off. She was making it on her own. On her terms.

She was happy.

"I don't party. I haven't been sleeping because I miss you."

She glanced at him out of the corner of her eye. "You don't miss me, you miss the sex. I was pretty phenomenal."

* * * *

Beck wanted to kiss the hell out of her and then throw her over his knee and spank her for her smart mouth. This wasn't going as planned. He was baring his goddamned heart, and she was supposed to have fallen into his arms by now.

"I love you," he barked.

"I'm needy."

"I need you."

"You don't want to need me. You can have

any woman you want. You're in search of peace inside a stress-free world of loneliness and repentance. That's an imaginary landscape that doesn't exist. You gotta have faith you are strong enough to deal." She sighed. Dark circles framed her eyes. "And you don't love me, Beck."

He ran his scarred hand through his hair. "I changed my mind!"

"You can't do that. Not where love is concerned. It's only expedient when choosing paint colors, picking out a tie, or ordering sushi if the fish doesn't look fresh."

In her yoga pants and an oversized MIT sweatshirt, her hair tied back in some flouncy ponytail and a set of black-rimmed glasses propped on her nose, she was beautiful. All her dignity…fighting against the small glimpse of vulnerability…

He wanted her with every breath in his body, with every aching pain from his past. A need so elemental he couldn't ignore it.

He was ready to forgive himself…for her.

"Listen to me!" He grabbed her and stopped her narrow escape. "I was scared. A coward, like you said. I didn't figure it out until after I got done being out of my fucking mind over almost losing you."

She waited, her big cat eyes staring at him like he was full of shit. "I'm more than capable of being responsible for my own life and death."

He sighed. "I went to the castle to regroup, to re-evaluate my life after rehab. And there you were. This gnawing, irresistible temptation that threw my peace and solitude into a state of chaos. And chaos means stress to me. I like to self-medicate when I'm under stress."

"Give it up, Slader. Truth is, you live on adrenaline. I am not adrenaline-producing material. You're addicted to being addicted, so you don't have to try living and possibly fail. I'm boring. Not addictive at all."

He stroked her cheek with the back of his hand. Hope flickered in her eyes, and he smiled. "I've found a new addiction. One that makes me a better person. One where I'm at peace within the chaos. You are my new addiction, Jude Duffy."

"That's only my oral sex skills luring you in. What if I die in your care?"

"I'll just have to jump into the grave with you." Beck grabbed her face in his hands. His heart swelled, but the battle wasn't over yet. "I love you, Jude. I want to be with you. No matter how long we have together."

She pulled her face from his hold and stared at the ground as she scuffed her small sneaker over the compact earth. "I'll have to think about it."

His heart plunged in his chest. "What's there to think about?" He didn't want her thinking. He only wanted her feeling. A thinking Jude meant trouble.

Her green gaze lifted to his. "What's in it for me?"

Insecurity settled over him. "Me?"

She snorted and stepped toward his right, circling him. "What else?"

"Anything you want." He turned, keeping her in sight.

She stepped closer. "A pool? A house with a pool?"

"Am I living with you?" He matched her approach, craving her touch, her scent.

She glanced away. "Maybe."

He reached for her hand, needing the connection. "Then yes, it's yours."

Her eyes slowly returned to him, a hint of

mischief in their depths. "What about porn? Can I have my porn magazines back? I'd like to continue my research."

"If you research only with me."

"Money. Can I have all your money?"

"It's yours."

She scrunched her nose. "Don't need it. Sex toys?"

"Don't need them. You got me." His fingers linked with hers.

"Almond Joys?"

"All you want," he whispered.

"Here's a tough one." She moved an inch closer, their chests almost touching. "What about a kid? Would you let me have a child?"

He smiled. "I can't imagine you without one. Mini Jude Duffys are needed in this world. Are we good now?"

She tilted that little red head of hers, examining him, evaluating him. "I suppose I'll take you back. But only under one more condition."

"Anything."

"I'll need help with a little research."

"What kind?"

"The kind that says I have to pee on this stick." She held up the pregnancy test she'd purchased at the drugstore on the way to her walk. "So, if you're gonna love me, Gabriel Beckette Slauter, love me like you mean it. If not, kiss me like I'm leaving."

"I'll do better than that."

Beck handed her an Almond Joy, picked her up and kissed the hell out of the one woman smart enough to save him from himself.

Take a sneak peek at Naima Simone's *Flirting with Sin*, the next novella in The Noble Pass Affaire series.

Flirting with Sin
A Noble Pass Affaire Novella

"Here we go." The concierge swung the door to the hotel suite open and Neveah rolled her eyes. Jesus Christ, he was so damn happy he practically chirped.

She followed him in and halted just inside the luxuriously appointed suite. Shock and pleasure rooted her feet to the floor, the same as it had outside the resort and in the lobby. Was there anything about this place not screaming history, wealth, and beauty? In the common area of the room, two large, high-back arm chairs and a wide, long sofa gathered around a huge fireplace, and mounted flat-screen television big enough to satisfy the manliest of man caves. An oak dining room table flanked by matching chairs decorated the other side of the open floor plan, while a surprisingly roomy kitchen occupied the farthest end of the room. A quartet of floor-to-ceiling windows granted a breath-stealing view of Lake Noble, mountains and the small village of Noble Pass in the distance. *Gorgeous*, she breathed. *Just gorgeous*.

"Here's your living and dining room combination. Of course, you have full access to the main dining room with all of your meals covered by the hotel. But, just in case you decide to eat in, you have a fully appointed kitchen. You have a tower suite, so there are two balconies. That door there," he pointed to a door she'd mistaken for a window, "leads to one, and there's another in the second bedroom." He waved a hand toward the closed door on the left side of the suite.

The closed door slowly creaked open, revealing the man she would be roomies with for the next seven days.

The rest of the concierge's spiel fell on deaf ears. She couldn't catch anything beyond the dull roar reverberating in her head like noise in an empty, vast cave.

Tattoos.

Lots of them.

They swirled in vivid tones of red, blue, purple and black from his wrists, up muscular arms to disappear under a dark, vintage AC/DC

T-shirt. More stark lines crept from under his collar and up the strong column of his neck. Most people would've probably called his skin "olive," but that would've been a misnomer. It was golden. As if God Himself had trapped liquid sunshine in His hand and created this man out of it.

Tearing her gaze from the strange allure of his throat, she dragged her study down his wide shoulders to his narrow hips and long legs encased in loose denim. He was tall, lean but with a whipcord power not unlike a very large predator.

Sleek, beautiful, controlled...*dangerous*.

She retraced her visual journey, eager to glimpse the face accompanying this body and rivaling the view outside the bank of windows. Jesus, he managed to pilfer her breath just standing there fully clothed. Naked, he would send a woman into a lust-induced cardiac arrest.

Now there was one for the medical journals...

Oh. Shit.

A sinful, carnal mouth was emphasized by a dusting of dark-brown facial hair above his top lip and along his chin and jaw...and the small, black hoop piercing one corner of his slightly plumper bottom lip.

A black baseball cap shielded his eyes, but she didn't need to see them to know they would be a startling shade of gold and green, exotic, unique. No, she didn't need to see them because the mouth was enough.

She could never mistake it. Hell, she'd stared at and fantasized about those sensual curves since she was eighteen.

"Hello, Mr. Riley." The hotel employee beamed, wielding his perpetual cheeriness on the tatted, pierced, brooding newcomer like a sledge hammer. "Your suite mate has arrived. I'd like you to meet Neveah Morgan."

Mr. Riley?

Suite mate.

Her heart pummeled her chest wall and the thunder in her ears grew louder, but for a different reason. Not nerves. But a very feminine fear and excitement.

And confusion.

Either the staff here was incredibly discreet or they didn't get out much. Or watch television. Or listened to the radio.

Because the last name of the man standing

several feet away from her, shoulders squared, arms crossed and feet spread in a don't-fuck-with-me stance, wasn't Riley. It was Sincero.

She closed her eyes, ordered herself to breathe and not run screaming out the door and hotel and down the mountain like a lunatic. Hysterics wouldn't serve to accomplish anything but a severe case of hypothermia. And with her return ticket home scheduled for next Monday—a week from now—and predicted snow possibly shutting down the mountain road, she was good and stuck.

Yup.

Thanks to her sister, it looked like she would be spending her vacation with a rock star.

Coming Soon from Josie Matthews
Crazy For Loving You

It's not every day a girl down on her luck gets to clandestinely watch her unrequited man-crush of fifteen years have animal sex on the kitchen island of his childhood mansion—a heck of a lot more entertaining than watching CSI reruns with her alcoholic, freeloading daddy in their doublewide. This must be Joley Rawlings' lucky day.

Then again, maybe not, since twelve hours later she almost got arrested for tasering his ass in the women's bathroom at the Love Bites Saloon.

Dylan Creed isn't going to be happy. But hey, it was worth it. And so is unexpectedly inheriting his father's minor league baseball franchise right out from under him.

So what if she doesn't know a Baltimore Chop from a pork chop. She'll figure it out, like she always does.

She has no choice.

About the Author
Josie Matthews

As a kid, Josie Matthews wanted to be Batman, but when she discovered his powers weren't

 real, she upped the ante for the DNA-enhanced Superman. It's a shame the tights were too small. Now, Wife Extraordinaire (snort) to a very patient husband and Mother ~~From Hell~~ of the Year (cough, cough) to two very appreciative boys, Josie lives, plays, and pays huge taxes in gorgeous upstate New York. Settling for college degrees (instead of the prohibitive tights) in computer science, then nursing, add a little side dabbling

in art and landscaping for the last thirty years, and she is finally zeroing in on what she wants to be when she grows up. Life is starting to get interesting and she's finally devoting time to her true passion—"Writing, will you please take fifteen steps forward."

Visit Josie at www.JosieMatthews.com or on Facebook or Twitter @JosieKMatthews any time to see what's cooking.

www.facebook.com/Josie.Matthews

www.twitter.com/JosieKMatthews